RAG AND BONE

KJ CHARLES

First published by Samhain Publishing. This revised edition published 2017.

Published by KJC Books

Cover design by Lexiconic Design
Interior design by eB Format
Swirl created by Alvaro_cabrera - Freepik.com
Edited by Anne Scott

Print ISBN: 978-1-9997846-5-2

With thanks to Amber Meadows. Cheers, mate!

CHAPTER ONE

It was a terrible day even before Crispin blew up the study.

It had started badly, as every day did under Mr. Maupert. He was not a patient teacher at the best of times; he specialised in resonance, a form of practice at which Crispin was embarrassingly inept; and after six miserable weeks of failure, it had become merely a question of whether teacher or student would crack first.

Obviously, that was Crispin.

He didn't mean to do it. He was trying his best, in the disheartening consciousness of his own uselessness; trying to ignore the constant nagging temptation of the better, easier, natural way. He was trying to get it right. So when Mr. Maupert shouted "Three over eight, boy!" Crispin tried to do that too.

He felt the power surge up his spine, flailing and uncontrolled. He pulled it into the best approximation he could of the pitch he thought Mr. Maupert wanted, saw the expression of open horror on his teacher's face, heard an unbearable high keening whine that he realised too late he had caused, and hit the floor with his arms over his head, on pure instinct, as every one of the glass bottles that lined the shelves exploded at once.

There were quite a lot of them.

The shattering noise was deafening but at least brief. The crash and tinkle of shards hitting the floor took longer. Then there was silence, broken only by Crispin's attempt not to cough as he inhaled the powder rising in the air.

He opened his eyes after a while, when it seemed safe, and peered up from behind the desk.

The floor was covered in glass shards and fragments, bits of dried plants, twisted stones, and a light coating of mostly brown dust that would become a lot thicker as the ballooning clouds of powder and spice subsided. The shelves were a twinkling mass of sharp edges. It would break Mr. Voake's heart, Crispin thought vaguely. What a lot of wasted bottles.

Mr. Maupert rose from a crouch as Crispin looked around at the destruction. His mouth opened and shut soundlessly for a moment.

He found his voice quite strongly in the end.

Crispin hurried unhappily through the corridors of the Council, holding a stinking bag of powder and broken glass at arm's length. He'd swept up everything else as Mr. Maupert shouted, trying to keep control because he was twenty-five years old, for God's sake, and he was not going to disgrace himself, but he didn't know how much more of this horrible, miserable business he could do.

He'd been retraining for seven months, he'd lost count of the failures and disasters in that time, and this was the third teacher who had given up on him. He was close to giving up on himself.

He needed to face the truth he had come to fear: he was too old to change. He'd grown out of shape, like a clifftop tree back home, so bent by the prevailing winds that it was permanently twisted sideways. That was what happened when you were taught everything wrong. How could he ever expect to put it right?

Crispin had been plucked out of his Cornish village, aged fourteen, by Mr. Marleigh, an elderly gentleman scholar who had spotted his burgeoning magical talents and selected him as his pupil, his successor. He'd been the kindest master, so patient, and Crispin had flowered under his tutelage. He'd known that their magical practice was technically illegal—well, Mr. Marleigh had openly admitted it—but he'd believed absolutely that it was not wrong, not *morally* wrong. *A mere quibble,* Mr. Marleigh said, *a matter of poorly phrased law,* and Crispin had accepted that without question because he'd loved him.

And then he'd learned that his teacher was a warlock, a murderer, and probably not even a person. The being he'd called Mr. Marleigh had been a human shell possessed by…well, *a pen* was the easiest way to put it, and all his kindliness to Crispin, over ten years together, had been nothing but getting a new body ready for when the old one wore out.

A decade of his life serving a cruel lie. That wasn't something that Crispin felt very good about.

He came to the imposing mahogany doors of the Council chamber. He hated those doors. Looking at them made him feel the way he'd felt seven months ago, when he'd been dragged in more or less under arrest to face days of interrogation. People, practitioners, had stared at him and whispered, *Warlock.* They still did that.

The doors were shut. He'd have to stand here until they were ready for him, whoever *they* were. Someone else to shout at him, probably.

The hall was high-ceilinged, hung with gilt-framed paintings. When the investigation had cleared him of deliberate wrongdoing, and decreed that he would be retrained to use his powers lawfully, he'd stood in this very hall, the headquarters of England's practitioners, looked at the grand figures of the past, and promised himself he would be one of them, one day. That felt like a bitter joke now.

He glared at the engraving of the Magpie Lord, the great lawmaker of centuries ago who had written the rules forbidding magic of blood and bone. The picture sneered back at him.

"Tredarloe." The voice was close to his ear, and Crispin jumped and turned, almost fumbling the stinking bag. He didn't want to drop it again; the reeking spice had been bad enough to clear up the first time.

It was Waterford, a student practitioner, accompanied by a serious young man who looked as miserable as Crispin felt. His heart sank. "What do you want?"

Waterford stepped forward so his companion couldn't hear. "Sorry to hear about your spot of *bother*, warlock." He spoke in the singsong voice of playground taunts although he was Crispin's own age, and he sounded absurdly nasal thanks to his badly broken nose, and anyway his own master had been part of a treasonous plot so he had no room at all to talk. None of that stopped Crispin cringing at the words.

"Just an accident." Crispin wasn't going to be bullied by Waterford; he was *not*. Ned wouldn't be. Ned would give as good as he got. Crispin wished Ned were here.

"Another one. Shame. You have a lot of them, don't you?"

"I'm trying to learn." Crispin stared over Waterford's shoulder, wishing he'd go away.

"Well, they shouldn't let you," Waterford said viciously. "They should have put you down with the rest."

"Oh, you can talk," Crispin hissed. "Your master—"

"*I* didn't help him," Waterford hissed back. "*I* wasn't a warlock, *I'm* not on watch. Even your precious justiciary decided I had no case to answer—"

"No nose, more like." That was childish, and Crispin felt embarrassed even as he blurted it out. It worked though, because Waterford went scarlet. He'd been egged on by his master to provoke the justiciar Jennifer Saint to violence, and he'd succeeded. The result was a flattened, bulbous nose that bent like a bow.

"You wouldn't be here now if you weren't the Yid's pet," Waterford spat. "It'll be different when we're rid of her and the dwarf. We'll see some changes around here then."

"If you can see past your nose," Crispin said, since he was being childish anyway.

Waterford gave him a look of pure hatred. "Warlock," he said again and turned away, jerking his head at his companion, whose impatience was becoming obvious. "Well, come on. Mustn't keep the *justiciary* waiting." He spoke with open contempt. Crispin rolled his eyes.

The problem was, though, Waterford was right.

Crispin had been cleared of active wrongdoing on the insistence of Esther Gold, senior justiciar, and against the protests of her opposite number, Mr. Macready, who had believed from the start that Crispin had been as bad as his master. But Mrs. Gold would soon be taking leave, whether temporary or permanent, to have her babies, and her partner, the short but terrifying Mr. Day, was to abandon the justiciary altogether, along with his junior, Saint. Rumour said they were to marry; certainly they were both wearing what looked like engagement rings. And six new justiciars were to be recruited to fill the empty posts and reshape London's justiciary.

If the new men—or women, of course—took Macready's side, if they weren't inclined to believe that Crispin was a reformed character, his position would be appalling. He'd be suspected at every turn, harried by people waiting for him to fall. He was already on a watch list and would be his whole life, probably, because everyone knew that once you'd tasted human blood and bone and the powers they gave, there was no leaving them behind, and no going back.

Crispin knew that better than anyone.

He jumped as the door in front of him opened, and an irritable voice called, "Tredarloe? Get in here."

Esther Gold sat at the Council table alone. She was doing a lot of that. It was called "filling in" because she was justiciary and not supposed to be there, but since one Council member had been decapitated in December and another shamed into resignation, she had been occupying one of the empty seats in a meaningful fashion. It was, she said, something to do with her time.

She was looking meaningful now, as well as enormously pregnant. "Tredarloe. Another day, another disaster."

Crispin looked at his feet.

She sighed. "This is probably my fault. I didn't think Maupert would be a great deal of use to you, but my options are limited, and I thought he'd be better than nothing. Clearly not." She exhaled through her nose, a harsh outward breath. "What the devil's that stench?"

"Oh. The bag. It, um… Some of the sweepings."

She sniffed lightly. "Wormwood. Lavender. Cedar, cinnamon— You brought this along because?"

"Mr. Maupert told me to."

"Any idea why?"

"No?" Crispin said helplessly.

"Because he was hoping I'd be sick on you, the malicious old goat. Get it *out*."

Crispin more or less ran to the door, dropping the bag outside, and returned to the table in somewhat less of a hurry. Mrs. Gold was looking sallow and breathing through her mouth.

"Everything stinks," she said, adenoidally. "I've spent six months either eating or being sick. One great big stomach, that's all I am. So, according to Mr. Maupert, you're making no effort to change your ways and you're an irredeemable warlock who ought to be on permanent watch for your inevitable fall. Comment?"

Crispin opened his mouth, groping for words. "I'm *not*." It sounded pathetically plaintive. "I don't mean to. I just can't do it. I have tried, I really have, but I can't do resonance because I can't *hear*. Everyone's trying to teach me different ways to work but—"

"But none of them are as easy as using the pen."

"It's not about it being easy," Crispin said, staring at the floor. "I didn't *expect* it to be easy. I'm prepared to work. But…if I don't use my powers any other way, and then I try to force it—"

"You get uncontrolled results. I know. Look at me, Tredarloe." She waited till he met her eyes. They were dark brown but not at all warm. "I think there is rather more to you than you're demonstrating. You've got a pronounced twist to your talents, there's no denying it. That happens. I've got damn all hearing myself, so I work with my nose—"

"I've got no senses at all," Crispin said bitterly. "I can't hear or smell or see, even."

"In an ideal world I'd pack you off for a month's intensive tuition with Stephen Day. He works with his hands, I'd wager he could find out what it is you should be doing. But since we're short-staffed as it is, *and* he's abandoning us to go off on adventures…" Mrs. Gold made a face. "The problem is, we all know you're a—" She clicked her fingers irritably. "Thing. Like the painter."

"Graphomancer." Very few people knew the word, since it was such an obscure talent. As far as Crispin could tell, the only ones anyone had heard of, other than him, were his corpse-raising, treacherous master and a recent notorious murderer. This was not auspicious company to be in.

"Graphomancer. And you will understand why that is not a popular thing to be."

"I don't kill people," Crispin said. "I have *never* killed people."

"No, but you certainly animated a dead one very effectively."

"That wasn't me!"

"Blood writing," Mrs. Gold said, ignoring him. "Soul writing. Like that maniac painter this winter who killed four officers of the Met. He drew them dead, and they did not make beautiful corpses. *And* he was from Cornwall. You run to warlockry down there, don't you?"

"That's just coincidence," Crispin mumbled.

"Statistics," Mrs. Gold said, adding something under her breath that might have been "yokels". "Appearances are against you, and I'm not going to be around much longer to fight your corner for you. You need to pull yourself together, you need to demonstrate some sort of ability to use your powers that doesn't make everyone else want to put their backs to the wall, and you need to do it quickly, because the number of people in this building who think you're worth the effort is a small and dwindling group."

Crispin knew he was bright red and his stomach was roiling miserably. He nodded because he didn't trust himself to speak.

"I do, however, have a new teacher lined up for you," Mrs. Gold went on. "Chap from Oxford, named Sweet, coming here to do some sort of research. Scholarly type, with an academic interest in graphomancy. He wrote to the Council to ask about you, in fact, so I thought we'd get some use out of him. I was planning to start you with him when he'd settled in, but since Mr. Maupert has declined to teach you again, you might as well go straight to Dr. Sweet. If I were you, I'd treat this as a new start. He's not London, he doesn't have every reason to distrust your sort, he might have a new approach. Go home, get some rest, be back here tomorrow at nine sharp to meet him." She cocked her head, fixing him with a shrewd, fractionally sympathetic look. "You're running out of chances, Tredarloe. Don't waste this one."

Crispin did go home, because he'd been told. He ran through the various exercises that he was supposed to do, washed his hands and changed his clothes in an effort to get rid of the smell of spices, and as soon as five o'clock approached, he did what he'd wanted to do all day, and headed for Grape Street.

It was a rancid little alley that didn't deserve the name of street, leading down to the fetid maze of St. Giles, certainly not a place that

Crispin would ever have wanted to visit without good reason. He wore his oldest boots, knowing the oily, sooty filth of the alleys didn't come off leather. At least he didn't have to pick his way through excrement: that was collected as soon as it fell. People on Grape Street couldn't afford to let anything go to waste.

The air was thick, as ever, with smoke and the smells of cooking, horse sweat, unwashed bodies and clothes, the rot of food too old even for the people here, and the prevailing odour of privies. That was the Grape Street smell, so strong Crispin could pick it up through the reek of spice that wouldn't leave his nose. The combination was impressively unpleasant.

Ned would probably not be back for a while yet, and although plenty of people lounged on the steps and against the walls of Grape Street, Crispin could not make one of them. He was clean, his coat had been bought new, and he looked like what the rookery dwellers would call a pigeon for plucking. Plucking was very much not what he'd come here for, so he didn't hesitate, but ducked through the door of Mr. Voake's rag and bottle.

The first time he'd come here, the rag and bottle (it was, for obscure reasons, a terrible faux pas to use the word *shop*) had seemed to be as crammed as any room could be. Now it was worse. Every vaguely level surface bore containers, every container was stuffed with rags, or with smaller boxes and bottles. Jars and jugs, barrels and caskets, metal and glass and wood and ceramics, all covered in a faint film of grease whose source Crispin had never identified, and coated on top of that with the relentless dust of Ned's paper store through the connecting door.

Mr. Voake, the rag'n'bottler (always to be said as a single, three-syllable word), was at his usual occupation of transferring piles of grey-brown rags from a sack to a drawer. In seven months Crispin had never seen him sell anything.

"Good evening, Mr. Voake," he said.

"E."

"Is Ned in, at all?"

"N."

"Mind if I wait?"

"G'o'e'."

Crispin decided that meant "Go on, then". He had privately concluded that Mr. Voake did not suffer so much from a speech impediment as from advanced lack of interest in his fellow man, which left him unable to summon up the energy to move his lips.

He drifted around the shop, trying to keep his coattails from touching things. It was a rather cheap coat, the one he always wore to come here. Anything he wore to visit Ned ended up puffing clouds of dust for days after, and in any case it seemed rather pointed for him to dress expensively when Ned owned one coat, one waistcoat, and two shirts. Still, just because it wasn't his best didn't mean he wanted to cover it in stickiness of unknown origin, and he certainly didn't want to send bottles crashing to the floor with an unwary movement. He'd done quite enough of that.

A high-pitched shriek from outside pulled his attention away from his problems. It wasn't an actual shriek; those were usually from the ragged children who swarmed the streets in packs. It was, rather, the tortured sound of a handcart's axle, and Crispin could tell that handcart from any in London.

He'd have liked to run out of the shop in greeting and fling himself into Ned's arms for a hug. Instead he lifted a hand to the dark, blurred form he saw through the dusty bull's-eye windows, and watched him pantomime a distorted response.

Ned was back, and Crispin could feel his shoulders sag as the tension finally started to dwindle. He waited impatiently until the badly fitted door that connected the rag and bottle to Ned's paper store shook and shuddered and was forced open by Ned's powerful shoulder, and hurried through to see his lover grinning broadly, waiting for him.

"Freckles," Ned said, locking the door. "You're a sight for—What the heck is that smell?"

They got in hot mutton pies from the shop on Dyott Street that Ned supplied with waste. It was easier than going out to eat, and more discreet, considering everything they couldn't talk about in public.

"So I have to see if this new teacher will be any good," Crispin concluded his lengthy monologue. Ned had listened patiently, as he always did. "Or, if I'll be any good, more like."

"I don't get it." Ned brushed crumbs off his trousers. They were both sitting on stacks of waste, using the piles of manuscripts, letters, prospectuses, and forgotten legal documents as furniture because Ned had neither the space nor the funds for things like chairs. He had a bed, a gimcrack chest of drawers, incredible amounts of paper, and very little else, and he was the most contented man Crispin knew. "I've seen you do magic. We both know you can do magic."

"I can. But…" Crispin had tried to explain this more than once. "Look, you're a wasteman. You know how to buy waste, how much to pay, who to sell it to, how to turn a profit. Well, suppose I told you to get on the Stock Exchange and make a fortune? It's all buying and selling, isn't it? You know how to do that, so why couldn't you do it with stocks and shares?" He gave Ned a hopeful look.

"I probably could," Ned said. "If I learned the rules, and if they let my colour into the Exchange, which I wouldn't bet on. I wasn't born a waste-man, or even bred one. You learn things."

Crispin sagged. Ned probably would make a marvellous stockbroker, if it came to that, because he was actually good at things. "Yes, well, I *was* born with my talents, or lack of them, and the way I was trained to use them isn't allowed, and I'm no good at learning the new way. I simply can't make my powers do what I want in the way people want me to. I mean, do you think you could ever learn to draw?"

"No," Ned said without hesitation.

"You could take lessons. If you had dozens of lessons, I bet you'd be able to turn out a reasonable likeness, but—"

"Not like you."

That was something Crispin *could* do. He'd sketched Ned half a dozen times, and himself in the mirror too, on request. Ned had that picture pinned to the wall of his tiny sleeping space. "No. I can take a pen and know how to put what I want on the paper. I can look at you and see how I'd shade your cheekbones in this light, how I'd draw your eyes." It was the laugh that made Ned's eyes, the little telltale crease there half the time even when he didn't seem to be smiling. When Crispin shaded his work, seeking to make his pencil's grey suggest the rich deep brown of Ned's skin, he found himself drawing as though Ned's eyes cast their own light.

Those eyes were on him, warm with amusement, and Crispin realised his fingers had adopted a writing position. He straightened his hand with a touch of self-consciousness. "But even if you tried and tried, it wouldn't come naturally, or easily. You'd never be able to do what I can do like breathing." Ned shrugged acknowledgement. "And now imagine you *could* draw beautifully if you did it a different way but you're not allowed."

Ned put an arm round his shoulders. His arms were glorious, thick with muscle, so Crispin had to incline his head to make room. He put up his own slim arm to take Ned's hand.

"I hear you," Ned said. "But you aren't allowed. So it seems to me that you've got to do it how they want you to."

"It's not fair." Crispin scuffed the paper dust on the floor, with his boot. "Just because a maniac used graphomancy to kill people—"

"You talking about your Mr. Marleigh, or the one who murdered a pack of peelers this winter?"

"The one this winter."

Ned sighed. "Missing my point there, Freckles. Be honest, I don't much like the sound of magic writing or the look of it either. I don't want you doing stuff with your own blood, let alone someone else's." He tugged Crispin's hand forward so they could both see the truncated little finger. "Don't tell me anything that starts with chopping bits off yourself is a good idea."

He sounded almost annoyed, and Crispin bit back an equally testy response. Ned didn't *know*. He was a waste-man, he didn't understand what it was like to have power. He didn't even want it. Ned was a flit, possessing a tiny touch of magical talent. He was just about able to hear the sounds of the ether to which Crispin was deaf, but he had steadfastly refused any suggestion of training his meagre ability. *Why would I hear more of that if I didn't have to?*

Crispin would have ki—would have done anything for the senses Ned didn't even want.

"Well, it's too late to change that," he muttered, pulling his hand back. "And I'm trying."

Ned squinted round at him. "That's as much as anyone can ask. Look, drop it for now, eh? I know you want to get this sorted out, but it's not the only thing in the world."

He was well aware he'd been talking a lot about it, until the twilight had shaded to night, but the implied rebuke was still galling. "It's the most important thing!" he retorted without thinking, and felt his stomach contract at the expression that crossed Ned's face. "I didn't mean— That is, it's what I *do*, it's the important bit of my *day*, not— Ned, I didn't mean that."

"Course not." Ned let his head drop back against the wall. "You want to stay?"

"Yes," Crispin said urgently. "I really do. I'll stop. Oh God, I haven't even asked about your day."

"Same old, same old." That proved Ned was offended: he never had a "same old" day. There was always a funny story, some observation or interaction turned into an anecdote, because Ned was interested in things, and people, and the world around him. He didn't only think about himself.

Crispin couldn't imagine why Ned put up with him.

He twisted to get his arms round Ned's muscular torso. "Well, if it wasn't a very interesting day, maybe I could make it more interesting?" he offered hopefully.

Ned let out a long breath. "Crispin…"

Oh, he couldn't have made a mess of this as well, not this. Crispin turned properly, swinging a leg over so he was sitting on Ned's lap, and took his face in his hands. "Please, Ned. I'm sorry. I've been looking forward to seeing you for days and now I've spoiled it. Can I start again?" He dropped kisses on Ned's cheekbones, one side and the other. "I'd rather be here than anywhere else, and I'd rather be talking to you than anyone else, and I'd rather you were talking to me and I wasn't talking at all because you make more sense than I do." He moved his mouth to Ned's jawline, over the rough slide of beard he'd grown through the winter and which Crispin had insisted he keep, down the side of his neck, and felt the paper dust slippery on his lips. "Please?"

Ned grunted, low in his throat, and his hands came up to Crispin's ribcage, sliding over his back. Crispin wriggled closer, kissing his way up Ned's throat and over his jaw until their lips met, and at last, for a little while, everything was all right again.

They ended up in Ned's tiny sleeping space, which didn't deserve the name of bedroom. It was a cubbyhole off the paper store, with a sacking curtain to keep the warmth of body heat in—Crispin still felt slightly embarrassed about the look Ned had given him back in the depths of winter when he'd complained the paper store didn't have a fireplace—with a truckle bed barely wide enough for the two of them lying on their sides. But Ned kept it swept and aired as best he could with no window, and Mr. Voake didn't notice comings and goings, or care if he did notice. It was a safe space for the two of them, a place where Crispin was himself. Not a practitioner, not a warlock, not a failure or a nancy or a molly or any of the other things he was outside. Just him and Ned, body to body, shivering under blankets that held the evening chill, warming each other up. Crispin couldn't wait for summer, the hot, light evenings when they wouldn't need covers and he could take his time looking at Ned's compact, powerful frame, and the sloping shoulders that made his mouth go dry.

Then again, burrowing under the blankets together had its advantages. Crispin wriggled on top of Ned's solidity, feeling his way by touch, exploring the wide chest with light hands. He hadn't expected Ned to be hairy, somehow, the first time, had had a vague idea that men of colour were smooth-skinned, and been pleased to find himself wrong about that. He rubbed his cheek against Ned's pelt, licking a nipple to attention, and felt Ned's solid thighs shift under him.

"You're all over, Freckles," Ned whispered, a laugh in his voice, and Crispin knew he was forgiven.

"I'll be all over you before long," Crispin assured him, and then they were both giggling like schoolchildren at the ridiculous innuendo. Crispin took the opportunity to squirm down a bit, and Ned shifted around, and there they were, with his prick caught between Ned's substantial thigh muscles and Ned's pressed along Crispin's belly, both of them rocking gently as Ned caught Crispin's mouth with his own.

Crispin was willowy, effete, his manner screaming *molly* no matter how hard he tried to hide it; Ned was strong-muscled, a working man, a black man. Both of them were very used to what other men wanted of them. And it had turned out Ned was as tired of those expectations as Crispin.

He pushed himself forward, finding a rhythm. Ned groaned into his mouth, moving to meet him, his skin hot and close around Crispin, his smooth, strong prick making its presence felt between them, butting up against Crispin's ribcage. Hands roaming, all four, both of them pulling against the other, Crispin fucking between Ned's thighs and Ned up against his chest, skin to skin, in glorious rhythm. Ned's mouth was so hot, so open, his hands slipping over Crispin's arse, his own clenching under Crispin's grasping fingers. He was moving harder now, faster, hips bucking, and Crispin could have been inside him for the tense flesh around his cock, the glorious pressure, for the sensation that Ned Hall of all the stunners wanted *Crispin* to fuck him—

Crispin yelped incoherently, feeling the waves of sensation through his cock and hips and skin, and came then, thrusting into Ned with urgent abandon, feeling the grip of his legs tighten. "Ned!"

"Ah, blimey. *Freckles.*" Ned's hands were clutching Crispin's arse, matching his rhythm, wringing every bit of pleasure out of him, until he was gasping, emptied, and spent.

Crispin let his head droop for a second, blinking away the spots in front of his eyes, and pulled away. He thrust himself backwards down the bed, his cock still rigid and aching, and gulped Ned's stiff length open-mouthed, like a trout to a fly. Ned cursed, hips lifting, so close that Crispin had only just got a satisfactory hold on him when Ned came too, his whole body locking with the effort.

Ned slumped back. Crispin slumped over him, face on his warm belly, legs dangling off the bottom of the truckle bed and sticking out into cold air.

"All over," Ned grunted, shifting what must have been uncomfortably sticky legs, and Crispin mumbled some sort of response, feeling himself at peace for the first time in a horrible, horrible day.

CHAPTER TWO

Ned woke up because of the singing.

That was the first odd thing. The paper store and the rag and bottle weren't far off Oxford Street to the north and St. Giles to the south. People outside the thin walls were singing at all hours, if they weren't swearing or screaming or selling things; a fellow who woke at every little noise wouldn't get a deal of sleep. Crispin said it had been months before he could sleep through the night in London. Seemed that in the countryside you only had owls and foxes and suchlike, making whatever noises they made. In London you had people and they didn't stop for night or day, and Ned had been brought up on the docks, where nothing ever stopped. He could sleep through anything.

But here he was, blinking awake in the darkness, with Crispin's body warm against him, breathing softly, and he could hear the sound of singing.

A deep, male voice. Ned couldn't make out the words, though it had the long, drawn-out plaintive notes of a country ballad, a vaguely familiar tune. And it was coming…

It was coming from the rag and bottle, through the door.

Voake? Surely not. Ned had been the rag'n'bottler's neighbour five years and was pretty sure he was the man's closest thing to a friend, but if they had an hour's conversation in a sixmonth it was more than Ned would expect. Even when Voake drank himself unconscious, he did it in grim silence, and on his own.

Which meant that some bugger had broken into the rag and bottle and was in there singing folksongs, which suggested a lot of drink. And Voake might be quiet but he wasn't deaf, so what the hell was going on?

"Gawd," Ned muttered, and pushed himself to a sitting position. He was on the wall side, with Crispin's slim but sleep-heavy body shoved up against him to avoid falling out of the narrow bed, and it was dark as the inside of a dog. He attempted to crab-clamber his way over Crispin without touching and promptly landed his knee on an unexpected leg.

"Wuh? Ned?"

Ned tried to ground his hand on the bed rather than Crispin, came down on what proved to be blanket without mattress under it, and lurched forward, hand hitting the floor with a jarring thump. Crispin yelped. "What are you doing?"

"Falling out of bed," Ned growled. "Make some light, will you?"

Yellow-green light bloomed around them, as though he'd put a match to gas. That was what Crispin called witchlight, one of the few forms of magic Ned could happily live with. When a man lived in a dry-rotted wooden house and a room full of old paper, he got to be wary of flame.

He clambered his way off the bed. Crispin was sitting up, blinking. "What on earth are you doing?"

Ned grabbed his drawers. It was blasted cold. "Finding out what that noise is next door."

"What noise?"

"The singing."

"*What* singing?"

"You deaf? That." It was really loud now, deep bass notes, and he could begin to make out words.

Tell her to wash it in yonder dry well
Parsley, sage, rosemary and thyme...

"Scarborough Fair!" Ned said, placing it at last.

"What?" Crispin repeated. "What are you talking about?"

"Can you not hear it?" Ned demanded, and stopped dead with his trousers round his knees, because if he could hear something Crispin couldn't—

The same realisation had evidently hit Crispin. "What are you hearing?"

"Deep voice. Bloke. Singing 'Scarborough Fair'. It's coming from next door. I thought it was a burglar."

Tell her to dry it on yonder thorn
Parsley, sage, rosemary and thyme...

Ned gave Crispin an expectant look. Crispin returned a plaintive one. "It's the middle of the night!"

Ned changed his look to a glare. The voice was soaring:

Which never bore blossom since Adam was born
And then she'll be a true love of mine.

"Oh, all *right*." Crispin swung his legs off the bed, looking rather dizzy. "But it—" His head went up. "What's that smell?"

Ned's sense of smell wasn't wonderful, he'd be the first to admit, breathing in paper dust all day and night, and there wasn't much you wanted to smell on Grape Street at the best of times so he didn't pay a lot of attention to what his nose told him. Plus, he'd slept with his face in Crispin's dirty-blond hair, which reeked of cinnamon and perfume and sour-sweet spices he couldn't name. It took him a couple of seconds to detect what Crispin was talking about.

"Smoke?"

"Fire." Crispin was on his feet, grabbing for his own trousers. "Ned, *fire*."

"Oh my days." Ned hauled his trousers shut and moved fast. There was no way out of his little bedspace but through the paper store, and that had no windows either, merely the bolted door at the back through which he lugged the waste in, and the door to the rag and bottle at the front. And it had been a dry spring so far, and everything he owned or cared about was right here in the paper store, and most of it was flammable.

He shoved the curtain aside and saw only darkness at first, which was a relief because his imagination had given him an inferno. Crispin's witchlight bloomed around him, and Ned snapped, "Douse it!"

"What—" Crispin said, but did it.

"There." The door, the sticking, ill-fitted door to the rag and bottle, was faintly outlined in orange, its flicker just visible. "It's next door."

"Can you still hear the singing?" Crispin demanded. He was scrabbling around in the dark, getting dressed. "Can I do light now?"

"Yes to both. It's louder." The voice was clear as a bell, singing the tune that was meant to be wistful with a dark, joyful relish. And a country accent to it, Ned was sure.

Ask her to do me this courtesy
Parsley, sage, rosemary and thyme
And ask for a like favour from me...

"Loike faverr", that was how it sounded. Not quite Crispin's accent—he came out like a right rustic when he wasn't watching his words—but not a hundred miles off, either.

"What on earth is going on?" Crispin demanded, sniffing. "Is Mr. Voake cooking something? It smells like roasting meat."

"Why would he be..." A thought hit Ned with such horrific force that he felt all his skin rise to goose pimples at once. *"Light."*

Crispin illuminated the whole room in lurid yellow-green, responding to Ned's urgency. Ned was already unbolting the door, putting his shoulder to the too-warm surface with frantic fear. Two heavy thumps before he could work out if this was a terrible idea, and the door swung inward, with Ned stumbling after it into a sudden violent burst of heat that was matched by the roaring, deafening bellow of triumphant song in his ears.

Something was on fire on the floor of the rag and bottle. Something about the size of a pig and the same shape, something that blazed with a fierceness Ned had only seen in a burning tar barrel, and reeked of charring flesh…

"Oh bleeding hell," Ned whispered into the maelstrom. "Oh God, no."

The warped weird reflections of flames were dancing off every bit of metal and glass in the shop. He could hear the crackle and leap as they reached greedily out for fuel.

The rag and bottle was stuffed with dry cloth and old wood. It would go up any second, and if, or when, the paper store caught after it, he and Crispin were both as dead as the burning man on the floor.

Ned turned on his heel, ready to bellow a series of orders—*Get to the pump! Water! Raise the alarm!*—and found himself blocked. Crispin stood in the doorway, thin bare shoulders tense, frantically scrawling on a piece of paper that he held against the door.

He was writing with a silver pen.

Ned's mouth dropped open. This could not be happening. But it was, because Crispin gave a single gasp of effort, and the blaze of flame sucked into itself with an audible pop and was gone.

There was no singing. There was no burning. There was no fire. Only the sizzle of melting fat, the smell of scorched flesh and scorched wood, and the look of guilt on Crispin's face.

"I…" Ned couldn't manage anything else. The air was thick with grease and smoke, and a man was lying burned on the floor, and Crispin still had that sodding pen; he was using the pen that drank his blood and could steal his soul…

"What happened here?" he demanded, because he didn't want to start with that. "Is that Voake? It is, isn't it?"

"Oh God." Crispin's slim shoulders sagged as he looked down. "Oh, Ned, I'm so sorry."

"He's really burned." Ned felt a peculiar sense of detachment as he stared at his neighbour's incinerated corpse. It should have been horrifying, he had an idea that somewhere in his mind he *was* horrified, but there were some things, like dead people walking down the street, or men you knew sizzling on the floor like sausages, that a fellow couldn't quite look at head-on without a bit of a run at it. "Where's he burned *from*? What happened? I mean, the shop—but a person can't just catch fire for no reason."

Crispin was looking round. It was warm in here, obviously, but his arms were wrapped around his slim bare chest as though he was freezing. "I don't know. You hear of spontaneous combustion—"

"You what?"

"People just catching fire for no reason. I know of at least one other case in London, and that was a rag'n'bottler too, actually, now I think of it, but it happened decades ago. Um. What about the singing?"

"It's stopped. It stopped when you put the fire out."

Crispin turned in a circle, staring round the shop. "Blast it. If I wasn't useless, I'd be able to *see* something. I don't know, Ned. I've no idea."

"Well, what do we do?" Ned demanded. "I mean, something in here started singing and Voake's been…roasted, and what the hell do we do? Call the peelers? Your lot, I mean, your what-d'you-call-'em. Like Mrs. Gold."

"Justiciary."

"That's what we do, right? They'll be able to sort this out, won't they?"

"Oh yes," Crispin said. His voice sounded hollow. "They'll be able to look in here and probably see exactly what happened and where the power came from and what the singing was—"

"Well, that's—"

"And what I did."

"What you did," Ned repeated.

"That wasn't easy," Crispin said. "It was a lot of fire. The room probably stinks of, of—"

"Blood magic." Ned hated how that phrase had become so familiar. It oughtn't be familiar to anyone. "If we call for the justiciary, they'll see you did blood magic. And, what does that mean? We don't call them? We leave him there on the floor like an overdone chop? There was magic singing and he burned to bloody death, next door to me!"

"They will *know*!" Crispin shouted back. He was always pale, but he looked unhealthy now. "Do you know what they'll do to me if they find out I used the damn pen?"

"No, I don't! What?"

"I don't know!"

They glared at each other over the body. Ned's skin and lips felt greasy from the air in here, which was not something he wanted to consider at all.

"They all think I'm a warlock as it is," Crispin went on, quieter but no less panicky. "If they find out that—that—"

"That you are one?" Ned said, and felt a little stab of guilt as Crispin's face convulsed, but he was really angry, the kind of anger that made hurting someone seem like a good idea. "I don't know what to say to you. You said you'd stopped. You said you wouldn't do it any more."

"I couldn't think of anything else." Crispin's voice was a thread. "Can you not see I had to do something? It was an emergency—"

"Yes, it was. Nobody could've seen that coming. Out of the blue. And you were here to spend the evening with me, so why'd you bring the bloody pen with you?"

Crispin's lips parted. He didn't answer.

"You ain't supposed to use it," Ned said, except that apparently he was shouting, because he heard his voice echo off the hollow glass and tin around him. "What the *hell*? You're supposed to have killed it! You want to end up like Marleigh? What the bloody hell are you playing at?"

"Well, it's a good thing I didn't kill it!" Crispin shouted right back. "What did you want me to do about this, burn to death with a glow of virtue?"

"No, you carry on. Turn into some…*thing* like your old master did, why don't you? Make a brand-new pen to murder people with—"

"I used *my* blood!" Crispin yelled in his face. "Mine! Not anyone else's, and I'll do what I want with it!"

"Right, and you're going to tell your Mrs. Gold that, are you?" Ned demanded. "Trot off back to this new teacher and say, 'Changed my mind, doing it my way'? No wonder you can't get anywhere."

Crispin's mouth opened in shock and hurt. Ned set his teeth, stepping back. "You can't let it go." He felt extraordinarily weary all of a sudden. "Can you? And there's poor old Voake dead on the floor, but you don't want to find out what killed him because they might find *you* out. Go home."

"What?"

"I said, go home." Ned turned away.

"But—"

"He was my neighbour." He looked out through the bull's-eye windows into the blackness of the empty street. "He didn't talk to me much. I've no idea what his Christian name was. But he was my neighbour and something killed him. He *burned*, and for all I know, alive. So you get off now and I'll do something about this. You probably don't want people knowing you were here in the night anyway. Go on," he said over Crispin's attempt at protest. "Just *go*."

Crispin swallowed, throat convulsing, then turned. Ned stood in the rag and bottle with the stink of cooked man in his nose, staring down, listening to Crispin move around the paper store as he finished dressing in silence.

There was a flare of natural flame, and the witchlight vanished. Crispin came in to the rag and bottle to put the oil lamp he'd lit on a shelf. He gave Ned a hopeless, miserable look, and left.

Ned waited until he'd heard the paper-store door shut before he went through. He bolted it carefully behind Crispin, sat down on a stack of waste, and put his head in his hands.

The pen. The sodding pen, with its carved silver barrel and its nib made from the bone of Crispin's missing fingertip, and its writing in blood.

Crispin's old master had been enslaved to, or possessed by, a similar pen. It had sucked in the souls of its users and made them into…Ned didn't even know what it had been, some kind of life or half-life of its own. He'd seen a normal, unmagical man who'd used that pen and been possessed and destroyed by it. Ned had broken it under the wheel of a draycart, and Crispin had said he was going to break his own. He'd *promised*.

But he hadn't. He was carrying it around with him. All the time he was meant to be learning the right way to do magic, he had the sodding blood pen sitting in his pocket.

Trying, my arse, Ned thought.

He wanted to be angry. He *was* angry, in the same way he was horrified and sickened at what had happened to Voake, all of it bubbling away in the back of his mind till he could get a bit of space to think about it. Because right now he was mostly thinking about Crispin, and that terrified, guilty look, and how he'd known bloody well how furious and betrayed Ned would feel but he'd done it anyway…

…to save the paper store, Ned's business, his home.

"Oh my days," Ned said on a breath into the silence.

It wasn't as if he cared about whatever magical laws Crispin was breaking. They were breaking a few of the regular laws on their own time, and Ned well knew that just because people said a thing was bad didn't make it so. What frightened him was Crispin. What frightened him was, he'd met a body being used as a puppet, and looked into eyes that didn't belong in a human face, and if he ever looked into Crispin's marshlight yellow-green eyes and saw someone who shouldn't be there…

"Oh, Freckles," he said aloud. "You berk."

He shouldn't have kicked him out. That had been stupid, and unhelpful, and no way to talk to a fellow you…cared for, and as for *I'll do something about this*, he couldn't imagine what he'd had in mind. Like what, waste-man? Trot around to that red-brick building on Lincoln's Inn Fields where they'd brought him to ask questions about the pen business? *Scuse me, gents, I got a dead man burned up next door and magic singing, want to give us a hand with it? Yes, Ned Hall, I was the one here in summer—that's right, Crispin Tredarloe's mate. The warlock.*

He'd made a right dog's dinner of this, and he knew why. It was because he wanted to matter more than magic.

There was a piece of nonsense for you. A street trader with nothing to his name but a bed and a few hundredweight of waste, thinking he might be more important than powers that could set the dead walking. Crispin could command nature, he could twist a man's memories and control fire, and what could Ned do? Barter over ha'pennies, that was what, and he'd made a decent life for himself doing that, but really. Really? In the end, if you had to choose between powers most people couldn't imagine and a common trader, what would anyone pick?

Ned hadn't wanted it to come to a choice. He'd hoped it wouldn't have to, that they could spend time together and do their jobs apart and get on. Just chunter along, the pair of them, him and Crispin.

But Crispin *wasn't* getting on. He was trapped, and stifled, and frustrated, and when Ned had seen him writing with that damn pen, he'd felt a squirm in his gut that he recognised and didn't want to. It was the feeling he used to get when Pa reached for the square bottle of gin, and Ma would suggest that he'd already had a couple of pints and was he sure, and Pa would turn on her and ask if a man couldn't have a drink in the evening when he'd worked his fingers to the bone all day, and Ned would know what was coming next, every time.

He wasn't going to do that, watching the drunkard reach for the bottle, waiting for the inevitable, because Crispin's yearning for magic was stronger than whatever he might feel for an ordinary bloke like Ned.

He stood, shoving himself upright with an ungainly motion that sent sheets of paper flying. It was the middle of the night with a burned man on the floor next door, and he was sitting here thinking nonsense. There was damn all he could do until the morning, damn all to be done for poor silent Voake now or ever. He ought to go back to bed.

So he'd need to get the lamp and bolt the connecting door too, what with the dead body in the next room and whatever had been singing maybe still there. Ned hadn't thought that one through when he'd packed Crispin off and left himself here, alone in the dark.

"You're a grown man, Edward Hall," he said aloud into the silent, empty, scorched-smelling night. "You're not scared of—" *something that set a man on fire like he'd been doused in oil* "—a bit of singing, are you?"

And as if in answer, he heard a voice.

Ask him to plough it with a lamb's horn
Parsley, sage, rosemary and thyme
And sow it all over with one peppercorn
Then he'll be a true love of mine.

It was the same voice, Ned thought, through the paralysing fear. The same deep, rustic voice, but this time crooning, soft, so soft he doubted he'd have heard the words except that it was the dead of night, and it was once again coming from the rag and bottle.

He really wished he hadn't sent Crispin away.

So. He could leg it for the back door, make a clean pair of heels. But the oil lamp was burning in the rag and bottle, and what if the thing, the voice, the whatever it was, set fire to the building again?

And this was his home, his workplace. This was *not* somewhere stray magic was welcome to settle. If he wanted bloody magic in here, he'd have asked Crispin for it.

"Right, you arsehole," Ned said into the darkness. "Let's have you."

Ask him to reap it with a sickle of leather...

"Parsley, sage, rosemary and thyme," Ned came in loud as he could, his church-tuned baritone drowning out the other voice in his own ears, at least. "And I don't know the words, whatever whatever, then he'll be a true love of mine."

He took a breath and heard only silence. It lasted for at least thirty seconds, long enough to make him think, *Well, that shut* that *up,* and then it started again.

When he has done and finished his work...

"Sod your parsley, your sage, your rosemary, your thyme, and your watercress if it comes to that," Ned announced, stalking forward so his legs didn't wobble. "Where are you, then? Eh? Where are you?"

He crossed the threshold, which was the point he realised he should have unbolted the back door first so he could make a run for it if need be. Too late now. He skirted the charcoaled, not-looking-at-it remains on the floor and looked around in the smooth gold light of the oil lamp.

Then he'll be a true love of mine.

The song was coming from a shelf. It was coming, Ned realised, from a jug. He raised the lamp high to see.

He'd seen the jug before. It had been here years, to his remembrance—a stoneware bottle with a handle at the back, cast in a bulbous and irregular shape that swelled out from a narrow neck to a bulging belly and then dwindled to a base that seemed too small for stability. It was about nine inches in height, a rather drab grey-brown-yellow shade, and the surface looked as though it would be rough to the touch. The mouth was sealed with wax and string, evidently long gone brittle with age but still holding, and the neck was decorated by a crisp and deep-relief image of a bearded face.

It looked properly old, the kind of old that could be called antique, although Ned doubted it had any value, otherwise Voake wouldn't have owned it. And there was singing coming from it.

From the *inside* of it, because this close Ned could swear he heard an echo, like as if you were singing in a cellar.

Well, there was a thing.

He prodded it very cautiously. It felt like…well, like stoneware, that was all, a plain, cheap bit of fired clay.

Oh, let me know that at least you will try

Or you'll never be a true love of mine.

The singing stopped. Was that the end of the song? Would something else start?

If whatever this was intended to spontaneously such-and-such him, he'd forgotten Crispin's jawbreaking word, he didn't have any way to stop it. That being the case, he took the jug down from the shelf.

Nothing happened. He turned it in his hand and felt something inside shift. He gave it a cautious shake, heard the faintest rattle. A sealed jug, full of something.

He could break the seal, prise off the wax, and have a look inside. Or he could find a rusty hatpin and jam it into his eyeball, because that seemed about as sensible and, in his experience of magic, would probably be no more unpleasant.

He put the bottle back on the shelf, carefully. The base was small compared to its round belly, and he had a vivid picture of the damn thing toppling to the floor. He definitely didn't want it to smash.

Well, the singing had stopped, Voake was still dead, and Ned had no ideas to offer. "So unless you've anything to add," he said aloud, "I'm going back to bed."

Which he duly did and blew out the lamp too, because he was a grown man, and because singing jugs were an unknown quantity, but he knew exactly what an unattended oil lamp in a paper store might do.

It was a very, very long night in the dark.

CHAPTER THREE

Crispin's appointment with his new teacher was at nine. At four in the morning, lying awake after a long, cold, solitary walk to his room, he'd decided to be at the Council building when it opened at seven. That way he could talk to the justiciary, ideally Mrs. Gold but any one of them he could find, and start the investigation into poor inarticulate Mr. Voake's death, as he should have agreed to do last night instead of being a craven, selfish coward.

That was the plan. Unfortunately, he fell asleep in a morass of self-reproach, woke at half past eight, and was still running at full pelt through the black-coated legal crowds of Lincoln's Inn when the clocks were chiming nine. The ever-unhelpful doorkeeper refused to confirm that Dr. Sweet even existed, let alone where he might be, and by the time Crispin, sweaty and gasping, knocked on a small study door, he was twenty minutes late and his chance of making a good first impression was well and truly past.

A muffled voice invited him to come in. He pushed open the door and saw a room full of boxes, some books already shelved, and in the middle of it a tallish, thinnish, stooped sort of man with wire-rimmed spectacles and eyebrows roughly the size and shape of unkempt mice.

"Mr. Tredarloe, I take it?" He had a pleasant, educated voice, with a slightly soft *r*. "I'm Dr. Sweet."

"I'm so sorry I'm late," Crispin managed between heaving breaths.

"Were you late on purpose? Because you think this meeting is unimportant?"

"No!"

"Then think no more of it. Do sit down and catch your breath. I'm afraid it's still rather at sixes and sevens here, but I dare say your business is more pressing than any mere unpacking. Would you care for a cup of tea?"

Crispin mumbled thanks, sat on the edge of the chair, accepted milk and no sugar, and waited for Dr. Sweet to begin.

"Well," that gentleman said. "I should introduce myself, I dare say. I'm attached to the Special Studies Department at All Souls College, if you've heard of that? No? No matter. It's where the more academically minded practitioners tend to congregate, and I am very much one of those. I'm not a teacher—we don't have undergraduates at All Souls—and I'm certainly not a justiciar." He steepled his fingers. "In other words, Mr. Tredarloe, I'm not going to turn you in."

Crispin swallowed. "Turn me in? For what?"

"Anything," Dr. Sweet said patiently. "My understanding is that you've been taught a very specific style of practice from which you can't break free and which is, to say the least, discouraged. Now, I'm going to hypothesise, and please tell me if I'm wrong, that everyone here has been so busy telling you how you *should* do things that nobody has stopped to look at how you *can* do them. I wonder if anyone has sat down to examine what your talents actually are, and why your old master picked you, of all victims. I wonder if anyone's paid a lot of attention to *you*."

Crispin shook his head dumbly. Dr. Sweet sighed. "London. Everyone here is so relentlessly busy. And I do know that there's been a great deal of upheaval after the events of winter, but really, an ounce of prevention is worth a pound of cure."

"Sorry?"

"It's no good people telling you not to be a warlock. You were made one, made to twist a certain way, and you must be untwisted before you can walk the straight and narrow path, if you will forgive the mangled metaphor."

"Can you do that?"

"Oh, I should think so. With a certain amount of work, needless to say, but what's life without a challenge?" Dr. Sweet smiled, and Crispin found he was smiling back. "Now, tell me about it from the beginning."

Crispin had been interrogated for days after the events of the summer, but that had been as a terrified witness to crime. He'd talked about it sometimes since, to Ned, but not much. Ned had seen a man's body taken over by an animating spirit that had intended to claim Crispin for itself. How could he possibly make him understand that the inhuman predator had also been a kindly master, a teacher Crispin had trusted and loved?

He *couldn't* explain it, not to Ned, but Dr. Sweet understood. He nodded and asked questions as gently phrased as they were incisive, and within a few minutes, Crispin's words were racing as he spoke of the trust, the allegiance, the years of close association, the betrayal.

He'd been talking for perhaps ten minutes when Dr. Sweet passed him a pencil and a sheaf of foolscap.

"Uh…?"

"To occupy your hands. Nothing more, don't make notes. I merely want you to have something to do with your hands while you talk."

Crispin was a chronic doodler, habitually sketching little shapes and pictures in the margins of books and over any papers that came to hand. He wasn't sure what had betrayed it, but Dr. Sweet gave him a nod to keep talking, and so he did. His training. Making the pen, severing the top joint of his own finger for the nib—

"May I see it?" Dr. Sweet held out his hand.

Crispin didn't even question how he knew. He pulled the silver pen out of his pocket and passed it over.

"Mmm. Impressive work. Very much your own, that's quite clear." Dr. Sweet ran it under his nose like a connoisseur with a cigar. "Used recently. Yes, I can see it would be hard not to." He gave it back. "Go on."

"But…aren't you going to…"

"I believe we discussed this, Mr. Tredarloe. Carry on."

Crispin carried on. He talked about their work, writing scripted papers, Mr. Marleigh's research, about how the pen worked because Dr. Sweet actually *understood* graphomancy, about his own blind, deaf insensitivity to the ether, about it all. He talked until he felt dizzy and empty because it was past eleven and he'd missed breakfast, and Dr. Sweet sent for tea and a stacked plate of biscuits, and Crispin talked some more. By noon his throat was sore, and he'd cried a little bit, and he hadn't felt so unburdened in months.

"Well." Dr. Sweet leaned back in his chair. "Well, well. May I see the paper?"

"What—" Crispin looked down at the paper, which he'd completely forgotten about, and blenched. He'd drawn some of the carvings on his pen, and abstract doodles, he'd illustrated ornate words, and right in the middle of it he'd sketched Ned. Just his eyes, those laughing eyes that Crispin never wanted to see angry at him, or hurt by him.

Dr. Sweet took the paper. "Mmm. Mmm. Mr. Tredarloe, you're a graphomancer. There is absolutely no question. One practitioner may operate through sound, or touch, or smell, another may be able to see the flow of ether, a third might use…spices?" He sniffed in a questioning way.

"Accident in Mr. Maupert's study," Crispin mumbled.

"You act by writing. That is not a crime, and you are not a criminal. It is extraordinarily rare, and I am not surprised that the being you knew as Marleigh wanted you so desperately. What's wrong with you is that you've been taught to draw your power down the wrong way. Blood writing is impractical if you use your own blood, and illegal if you don't. But there are other sources of power, other ways for a graphomancer to work. Of course Marleigh did not teach you those; it was not in his interests to do so. I can."

"Oh God." Crispin's hands were shaking. "You mean it? You will?"

"My dear chap—may I call you Crispin? My dear Crispin, you are a rare and precious talent, a fascinating case study and, I think, a young man who deserves a chance. I should object in the strongest terms if anyone attempted to take you away from me now. Goodness me, I came to London to pursue my areas of interest; I had no idea such a plum would fall into my lap on the first day. I very much look forward to working with you." He extended his hand and Crispin, scarcely believing, shook it. "I really must get myself settled in, so we will begin tomorrow. Ten o'clock? Excellent. A very good day to you."

Crispin felt as though he floated down to the aggressively untidy area of the building where the justiciary lurked. He was usually horribly self-conscious about coming here, in case anyone thought he was being arrested. Not today.

A rare and precious talent.

He didn't want to spoil his mood by encountering Mr. Macready's hostility. Esther Gold couldn't actually work since her pregnancy prevented her from using her powers, and in any case she was nowhere to be found; Stephen Day was too senior, too busy, and far too intimidating for Crispin's liking. That left the junior justiciar Peter Janossi. Crispin knocked at his closed door.

"Come in, Tredarloe," Janossi called, because *he* didn't lack magical senses.

Crispin edged in. The room was, frankly, a dustheap, crammed with papers and dockets and boxes and bottles, all the paraphernalia of practice and of administration. It was approximately what would result if Ned's paper store mated with Voake's rag and bottle. Janossi stood with a huge armful of papers, attempting to flick through them while holding them in a way that Crispin suspected would not end well.

"What can I do for you?" Janossi asked without looking up. "Actually, you're a graphomancer. Can you find scripted paper?"

"Where?"

"Here." Janossi gestured with his armful to encompass the entire room's mess. The middle section of the sheaf slithered out with the movement and hit the floor in a whispering cascade. He swore.

"Uh, no, not really," Crispin said apologetically. "Not at all. I'm happy to help you look the normal way, if you like? But I wondered if you could come and help me with something first, please."

"Is it an important something?" Janossi said. "Because I am actually quite busy."

"Spontaneous human combustion?"

"I'll get my coat."

Crispin explained matters to Janossi on the way, giving a somewhat adjusted version of events. He had been visiting his friend Hall for a late drink when they'd smelled smoke, he said. He didn't mention using blood magic. Janossi, whose senses reached through walls and closed doors, would be able to tell he'd used it, no question. Crispin had decided the best way to tackle that would be to let him see the shop first. The scorched floorboards, the dead man, the paper store next door. Surely Janossi would be more sympathetic to his decision if he saw the evidence of its need?

That was what Crispin told himself, at least, though a little part of his mind was aware he was finding reasons to put the confession off.

The rag and bottle was closed up when they arrived. Crispin went round the back, to the paper store entrance, to see if Ned was there, and found the door unbolted and soft snoring emanating from the sleeping space. He called out, and Ned emerged after a few minutes, blinking.

"This is Mr. Hall," Crispin told Janossi loudly. "He lives here, and he saw what happened. Ned, this is Mr. Janossi of the justiciary. He's going to look into poor Mr. Voake."

Ned took a second to assimilate that, then he smiled, and the smile was enough to cement this as the best day Crispin had had in an age. It was forgiveness and pleasure and relief that Crispin had done the right thing, and he felt it wash away the horrible sick feeling of *not good enough* that built up in his gut. He…well, he liked it when Ned looked at him like that.

"I'm glad to see you, Mr. Janossi. Come in." Ned led the way. "Bit of a nasty business, as you see."

He pushed open the door, and Janossi went through into the cramped chaos of the rag and bottle with its stale cold-smoke smell. He looked down at the body on the floor. "Uh-huh. Is that meant to be human?"

"But it's tiny," Crispin said blankly.

"It was a lot bigger last night," Ned said over him. "I mean, it was person-sized. It *was* a person. Voake wasn't precisely strapping, God rest him, but what was left was a lot bigger than this."

"So, what, it burned away?" Janossi dropped to his knees on the greasy, sooty, dusty boards and prodded at the cindered remains. They were about the size of a small dog.

"Well, no." Ned frowned. "I went to sleep with the fire right out and the body, you know, human size. I came in this morning, and it was like this."

"Hmm." Janossi squinted around the shop. "You said singing?"

"There's the culprit." Ned indicated a jug on the shelf. "The noise was definitely coming from that. It sang while the body was burning, then again after. 'Scarborough Fair', it was, over and over. And I reckon it was, uh, magic sound."

Janossi's brows shot up. "Do you now?"

"He's a flit," Crispin said. "He's got a bit of hearing."

"And you can tell the difference between real sound and the other sort when you hear it, can you?" Janossi looked decidedly sceptical.

"Yes," Ned said. Crispin knew perfectly well he couldn't. "Plus, the noise came from inside the jug, no question, and I didn't see any ventriloquists hanging round."

Janossi considered that. He gave a one-shouldered shrug. "All right. 'Scarborough Fair', you say?"

"That's the one."

"Parsley, sage, rosemary and thyme," Janossi half-sang, picking the jug up. He shook it, squinted at it, and put it to his ear. "Well, that's odd."

"What?" Crispin asked. "What are you getting?"

"Nothing." Janossi turned it over. "Nothing off this, nothing in the room. I mean, I can see the dead chap, and a man doesn't burn to death in the middle of a shop by natural means, so I'm taking your word for this business, but for all the traces in here… I mean, there's nothing. Can you not tell?" he asked Crispin.

"My talents don't work that way."

"Hmph." Janossi squinted at the bearded jug. "You're absolutely sure the singing came from this?"

"I'm not an expert but that's what I heard," Ned said. "I'd swear to it."

"Know what it is?"

Crispin and Ned both shrugged.

Janossi propped himself against a chest of drawers. "It's a Bellarmine jug. Or Bartmann jug, some people call them, because of the face. Bartmann, bearded man. It's a witch bottle."

"Good grief," Crispin said. "Really?"

"What's that, then?" Ned asked.

"Oh, very old practice. You know something about this sort of thing, right?"

"Me?" Ned said. "No."

"He was involved in my, uh, trouble back last summer," Crispin offered. "With the scripted paper. But only by accident."

"You're the waste-man," Janossi said. "I remember. I was a bit busy that day, dealing with the walking corpse Tredarloe had loose. Often find yourself mixed up in trouble, do you, Mr. Hall?"

Maybe it was Crispin's general sense of guilt that made the hair on his neck rise at Janossi's tone. Or maybe it wasn't, because Ned's broad shoulders set in a way that Crispin didn't often see.

"Not sure what you're getting at there, mate." Ned's voice was very even. "I wasn't mixed up in the last business except that I bought the wrong stack of waste, and I'm not mixed up in this because, like you say, this was done with magic, which is your business, not mine. Often find yourself in trouble, do you, Mr. Janossi?"

There was a fractional pause, then Janossi nodded. "Fair enough. Well, witch bottles. Old business, very old. I don't suppose anyone's done this in a hundred years or more, but it used to be a popular sort of standby. If you were attacked by a practitioner—a witch or warlock, they'd have said in those days—you'd get a bottle much like this. You can use any kind, actually, but your Bellarmine jug is traditional, and tradition's important with sympathetic magic. Pop in a handful of pins and nails, plus—well, you know the sort of thing. Rosemary needles, grave earth, white sand, bone ash."

Crispin nodded understanding, attempting not to look at the disgust on Ned's face.

"The afflicted fills it up with piss. Seal it, chuck it on the fire, and Bob's your uncle." Janossi squinted at the ancient wax and string over the bottle's mouth, and gave it a shake. "Doesn't look like this ever got put on a fire, mind, but it's full of something that sounds like nails and pins. I suppose the piss has evaporated by now. Is stoneware porous?"

"Hold on," Ned said. "What do you mean, Bob's your uncle? You piss in a bottle and throw it on the fire, and what happens then?"

"Well, it draws the witch," Janossi said, rather brusquely. "The hotter the bottle gets, the more it hurts him and the harder he's summoned, till he's dragged to your door in agony. This is proper old-country stuff, you see, how people used to deal with trouble themselves. These days you've got the justiciary to come round and make you sorry you were ever born. The march of progress." He smiled at Crispin without mirth.

"Right, so what does all that mean?" Ned demanded. "Why was it singing, and what the hell did it do to Voake?"

"As far as I can see, nothing." Janossi put the bottle back on the shelf. "Mr. Hall, with the best will in the world, you're not trained, you've no power to speak of, and you don't know anything. This is an old witch bottle, and if it ever had any power to it in the first place, it's been dead and gone for a hundred years or more. There is *nothing here*."

"Except the dead bloke."

"Granted, yes, but what there *isn't* is the faintest trace of anything in the ether," Janossi said patiently. "It's clear as glass. Believe me, if any sort of practice had taken place last night, I'd see it, but it didn't. The bottle's inert. The room's empty. There's been no magic done here at all."

"No magic done," Ned repeated. He wasn't looking at Crispin.

And Crispin really had to say something, he had to say, *Are you joking, I used blood magic to put out a small inferno less than twelve hours ago, when I was here in the middle of the night…*

But he didn't, and nor did Ned.

"Spontaneous combustion," Janossi said. "I can't see what else it could have been. There's no trace of magic, and you can't burn a man on a floor with no fuel. It was spontaneous combustion."

"So what caused it?" Ned demanded.

"Nothing. It was spontaneous." Janossi shrugged. "Natural phenomenon."

Ned's eyes narrowed. "I don't have your education, Mr. Janossi, but it sounds to me like you're saying, *it just happened*. Which ain't an explanation in my book."

"I don't owe you an explanation. It's a very unusual thing, and sometimes very unusual things happen. He was a drinker, yes? There was a case a few years back, another rag and bottle seller—"

"Yes, I heard," Ned said, somewhat irritably. "What am I supposed to tell the crowner, then?"

"I'll send someone for the body. Remains," Janossi amended. "No point causing trouble. Did he have any relatives?"

"Not to my knowledge."

"Good. Leave it with me. Don't worry, though. There's no sign of anything gone on here at all."

CHAPTER FOUR

Janossi left. Crispin and Ned stood in the shop and stared at each other.

"No magic," Ned said at last.

"I don't understand." Crispin worried at a ragged thumbnail. "I mean, he's a junior, but everyone says he's competent, and he's got superb sight. He saw me through a door earlier. How could he not tell I'd used the pen? And what happened to Mr. Voake's body?"

"Blue-blasted if I know. It was like that this morning. Come here." Ned took his hand and tugged him into the paper store where they were private. "Freckles, listen. I'm sorry I shouted at you—"

"No, you were right. I shouldn't have—"

"Shush a minute," Ned said firmly. "I'm sorry I shouted, *but*, I want you to break the pen."

"You—?"

"It's got to go. Now. I don't want it sitting in your pocket where you can reach for it. I know you used it to save the store, and I'm thankful for that, but I don't want to see you arrested, and I can't see you end up like Marleigh." Ned's expression was raw. "I was up all night thinking about this. Well, this and whether that damn singing thing was going to set fire to me, but the point is, I'm scared. I'm scared for you, and I'm scared that we're stood here with Voake burned on the floor next door and the peelers aren't looking into it because we didn't tell 'em the truth. If you'd said, *hang on, I used my blood pen—*"

"I know," Crispin muttered. "I *know.*"

"Yes, well, I didn't say it either. We both hid it because we didn't either of us want to see you in chokey, so your justice man thinks there's nothing going on, and what do we do now?" He sat heavily on a stack of waste. "I know you want your magic, but I'm not watching you keep that blasted pen on you, and that's the long and short of it. I don't like this road, and I'm not watching you walk down it. Maybe I can't stop you, but I'm sure as blazes not helping you. So…I want you to break it."

Crispin swallowed, biting back, *Or what?* Was this an ultimatum? He couldn't tell and didn't think he wanted to know. "Ned, listen. I had that meeting today—no, this is relevant, please listen." He gave a very brief summary of what Dr. Sweet had said. "He thinks that he can teach me properly. I mean, he *listened.* And if that's the case, well, I won't need the pen."

"You don't need it anyway."

"I do," Crispin said. "I can't *not* do magic. I can control my powers with the pen in a way I can't otherwise. If I break it before I can use my powers in a controlled way, I might use them in an uncontrolled way and that's not good. Or if I need to—" He abandoned that line of argument at Ned's look. "But I don't want to break it yet, in case this doesn't work with Dr. Sweet."

Ned made a throaty noise of exasperation. "Right, but when won't there be an *in case*? When won't there be a reason?"

"When I've learned to do without it!"

Ned considered. "All right. Hand it over."

"What?"

"Give it to me. I'll hang on to it. You need it again, well, talk to me. But that way I'll know you're not using it." He met Crispin's gaze levelly. "I got to know."

Crispin could feel himself flushing. The shame thickened his throat. "I'm not a child. I wouldn't—"

"Lie about it?"

That hung in the air. Crispin knew damned well that if he hadn't precisely lied, he'd certainly omitted, and maybe misled. Ned was probably right to feel he couldn't be trusted.

He didn't want to give the pen up.

He didn't want to with a whole-body reluctance. It was his power, his past, his *finger*. It was what he could rely on when all else failed. It was his blood and bone. Ned didn't, couldn't understand.

But Ned's brown eyes were implacable, his lips set. He wasn't a fool or a coward: his calm good sense was all that had kept Crispin going at points. And he'd let himself down in front of Ned only last night. How often could he do that before his lover turned away?

He fished the pen out of his inner pocket, feeling the carved silver surface cool and familiar under his fingers, and handed it over.

"I'll keep it safe," Ned said gently, slipping it into his own inner pocket. "Thanks. C'mere." He stood, stepping forward, and Crispin came into his arms, resting his head on Ned's shoulder, feeling the familiar rough, dusty cloth against his cheek. "Ah, Freckles. This is hard on you, ain't it?"

"Not feeling very chipper," Crispin mumbled into his neck. That was Ned's word, and he felt him shake on a laugh.

"No, I bet." Ned's arms tightened. "Just—look, let's get this said. What about Voake? Can you make your man Janossi come back? I mean, if you said about the pen and explained…"

"But what would he do?" Crispin straightened. "He already looked, and he couldn't find any evidence of anything."

"Why not? Because, even if poor old Voake was a natural phenomenon, we know flaming well you did blood magic. So why didn't he see that?"

"That's a very good question," Crispin said. "I don't have the faintest idea of the answer. Maybe whatever causes spontaneous combustion hid what I did?"

"Umph." Ned chewed his lip.

"I don't think Janossi's going to be much more help now. The justiciary are in rather a state, and he's busy." And, quite clearly, the justiciar had not liked Ned's persistence. Crispin had seen that a couple of times. Mostly, Ned's even-tempered cheerfulness set the tone of conversations, but there were men who bristled a little for reasons Crispin could never quite identify, as if Ned were some sort of challenge, or threat.

Crispin was no threat at all, and he had offered to help Janossi find his lost paper. If he did that, perhaps he could get on the man's good side.

"I'll talk to him," he offered. "See what I can do. I won't let it go without asking more, Ned, I promise."

"What about that jug?"

Crispin shrugged, feeling the weight of Ned's arms with the movement. "Look, whatever else, I'm sure Janossi would have noticed if it was doing anything. Do you want me to get rid of it?"

"Eh, I dunno. It belongs to whoever owns the shop now, can't just chuck it away. Unless you think it's dangerous? It's been here for ages and nobody's ever spontaneously whatever-it-was before, but…"

"I honestly don't know. Janossi said it was inert. I suppose it might have sung in response to whatever was happening. Picking up whatever was in the ether, do you see? If there was power washing around for it to tap in to for a while…"

"Right, I get you."

"I don't know," Crispin said again. He wanted to say he knew. He would have liked to deal with it all, to remove the little lines of worry from Ned's tired eyes. Or to announce firmly that Ned would be coming to stay with him until such time as they understood what the devil had happened here and could be sure it wouldn't happen again.

No chance of that. Crispin had a small room in a lodging house, without so much as a parlour to sit in. The landlady did not permit guests for more than half an hour at a time; he couldn't imagine her reaction if he brought a dusty labourer home to sleep on his floor. And there was no point telling Ned to go somewhere else because he *had* nowhere else. This was his home and his business, his life. He didn't have a family. He had a lot of friends, and all of them were as poor as church mice, just as he was. London was crowded with the desperate and the struggling; being fussy about where you slept was a luxury most people couldn't afford.

Crispin exhaled, feeling his breath bounce back at him off Ned's warm skin. "What a day. Days."

"Mmm. Never a dull moment with you." The affection in his voice told Crispin he'd been forgiven, and the relief was so overwhelming that he had to shut his eyes.

"It's not my fault." Since his mouth was so close to Ned's shoulder anyway, he darted his tongue out and up the side of Ned's firm neck, tasting paper dust. "Pure coincidence." He licked Ned's earlobe, felt his arms tighten responsively. Ned had a bit of a weakness for ears. Crispin nipped at the lobe, rolling it gently between his teeth, and heard a low groan.

Ned's hand moved, sliding down the curve of his spine. Crispin had a nervous twitch, jolting away when the small of his back was touched. Ned knew it perfectly well and had his own hips right there, ready to meet the involuntary thrust. Crispin grinned against his skin, making the movement deliberate, and felt Ned's hands closing over his arse.

Ned was angling his neck. Crispin took the hint and kissed his way to the hollow of his throat, tracing the rounded ends of his prominent collarbones with the tip of his tongue, and as he did it, he moved his hands behind his back to trap Ned's, interlacing their fingers. Ned's Adam's apple shifted as he swallowed. Crispin teased it with his tongue, working his way up under Ned's bristly chin, making him squirm with a combination of ticklishness and arousal that Crispin adored. Ned was so self-reliant, so strong and solid and resilient; it made Crispin's insides turn over when he got at the vulnerable spots.

He pushed Ned backwards to the tiny sleeping space, the pair of them moving together with hands still interlocked. He'd have liked to push him right back onto the bed, but Ned was a sizeable man and one corner of the truckle bed was already held up with a stack of paper from when they'd done that too enthusiastically before. He made himself move with a bit more care, nipping and nibbling at Ned's jawline, lips, and ear as they both wriggled into a comfortable position, Ned on his back and Crispin over him.

"Ah, Freckles. You're gorgeous." Ned had his hands free now, both of them in Crispin's hair. Crispin trapped one and pulled it round to his mouth. He loved Ned's hands. They were capable hands: rough, a bit battered, with an old scar over a couple of knuckles. The sort of hands that kept you safe, the sort you could trust.

Crispin planted a kiss in the middle of Ned's palm, traced his tongue up to the web between two fingers, licked between them with deliberate pressure and felt Ned's hips undulate. The ever-present paper dust was dry on his lips, and he paused to wipe them, contemplating the sides of Ned's palm and fingers, where brown changed to pink. "Why are your palms paler than the rest of your hands?" he asked, idly tracing Ned's heart line with a fingertip.

"Dunno. Same reason you've got freckles, probably."

"Why's that?"

"Dunno."

"Well, I do," Crispin said. "It's to get handsome men excited."

Ned raised a brow. "Men?"

"You."

"Better." Ned's hands closed on his waistband, tugging gently. "Talking of excited…"

"You stay there." Crispin shifted back so he was kneeling over Ned, and stroked a hand over his substantial arousal. Ned's mouth opened in silent pleasure. Crispin took his time, undoing buttons slowly and teasingly, watching Ned's face with a heady sense of power along with his own building pleasure. Ned wore an almost-stunned look when Crispin made love to him like this, as if he didn't quite believe it, and it was about the only point in their relationship where Crispin felt as though he was leading.

Not that he wanted to lead, as such. He just didn't always like to be lagging behind, the one who needed a helping hand.

Talking of which. He curled the fingers of one hand around Ned's cock, rubbing his thumb gently over its ridges and veins, loving the way Ned's breath caught. He slipped the other hand between Ned's thighs, stroking coarse hair and smooth flesh, tracing a finger over the cleft of his powerful arse. That was as far as he'd go. Neither of them particularly enjoyed buggery—Crispin's few attempts had hurt like hell, and he'd been relieved to learn Ned was no keener—and who needed it when he could drive Ned out of his mind with the lightest strokes and touches?

Ned's abdominal muscles were clenching, his whole body tense with anticipation. Crispin took another moment to admire the view, then leaned forward to take Ned's prick in his mouth.

Ned made a strangled sound. Crispin didn't go wild, merely held the tip between his lips, sucking gently in a pulsing, loving rhythm until Ned was gasping and moaning with every flex of Crispin's mouth. He went to work then, taking him down as far as he could, with long strokes of his lips and both hands working between Ned's thighs, until Ned shouted with inarticulate pleasure and came, spending in Crispin's mouth with a soul-deep groan.

Crispin swallowed and leaned forward to claim a kiss, or rather to deliver one because Ned's mouth was slack. "There we are."

Ned made an inarticulate sort of sound and lay for a moment before working up the strength to get his arm over Crispin's back. "You're getting good at that."

"Practice makes perfect."

"Don't let me stop you." Ned's eyes looked heavy. "Return the favour," he added. "Give us a second."

"No hurry." Crispin wiggled himself to a position slightly less on top of Ned, and was unsurprised when his breathing changed within minutes to the rhythm of sleep.

He lay, listening to Ned breathe and relishing the moment. This was indeed perfect. Except for his own painfully rigid erection, of course, but Ned would take care of that when he woke; he had a habit of falling asleep directly after climax that Crispin found peculiarly endearing. But it was perfect anyway, as it always was in here. They could talk and make love with such uncomplicated joy. Crispin could make Ned happy simply by being here.

And then they left the little room, and Crispin's consciousness of his own failings and inadequacies would creep up on him again.

He knew Ned was fond of him, outside the fucking. That was obvious, and he wasn't so self-loathing as to tell himself otherwise. But *fond* didn't mean blind to his faults. Very much not.

The truth he didn't want to face was, Ned had taken his pen because he didn't trust Crispin with it. He, like the Council, like Mrs. Gold and Waterford and Mr. Maupert and everyone except Dr. Sweet, believed that Crispin would always fall back on blood magic. That, in the end, he was a warlock.

Logically, he knew Ned was different. He didn't know what warlockry meant, or understand magic of blood and bone; he'd taken the pen out of fear for Crispin, not fear of him. It still showed Ned didn't trust him, and the shame of that was something Crispin's mind flinched from. How could he have made such a mess of things that Ned, of all men on earth, didn't *trust* him?

He had to be trustworthy, it was as simple as that. He had to show he didn't need the pen, that he could put the work in and stand on his own feet. Dr. Sweet had said he could; well, he damn well would.

Because Ned was solid, Ned was reliable, Ned was trustworthy, and if Crispin couldn't be those things, he was very afraid that what he was simply wouldn't be good enough.

CHAPTER FIVE

"Pleasure doing business with you." Ned gave his cap a courteous tug, waved farewell to the Soho Bazaar's waste-buyer, and trundled the handcart, with its usual screech, off down Soho Street.

He was tired after a long day's waste-hauling. It was quarter to three and he'd been up since six, back and forth to the store four times, buying and selling. He fancied a sit-down, a mug of coffee from the stall on Soho Square to wet his whistle, maybe a bit of backchat with the merry Frenchy who ran it. A rest.

Soho Square was a comfortable place for that. A bit of green in the middle of the heaving smoke-black city, with trees and grass and a few flowers coming, and some benches where a fellow could rest his legs. And it was…what was Crispin's word for it…cosmopolitan. That made Ned think of *cosmic*, of the great wide sky you could see if you got up over London's rooftops, and he supposed that was what it meant. Soho was full of Frenchies, refugees and communards and whores; restaurants and laundries and churches and tailors. Germans too, lots more of them, Jews and otherwise, bakers and bootmakers. Italians everywhere, like the wizened old fellow playing his hurdy-gurdy while a black-eyed boy danced for coppers. Indians, now and then, in suits mostly, sometimes a fellow in brighter foreign garb. Men of colour.

The point was, everyone here was from somewhere else, one way or another, and none of them were inclined to make a fuss about it, and a fellow could sit on a bench, minding his own business, without getting *looked* at. Ned stretched his legs out, leaned back, checked to be sure Crispin's pen was still safely in his pocket, and gazed up at the budding leaves, thinking.

It was a good ten days since he'd taken the pen off Crispin and, to give him his due, he hadn't asked for it back. At first Ned had kept it on him because, and he wasn't proud of this, he'd not been quite happy to let it out of his sight. In case—you know. Just so he could be sure Crispin didn't happen to pick it up. Then, when it had become apparent he didn't need to be such a suspicious so-and-so and could leave it somewhere, he'd not had a clue where. He didn't have a strongbox or a safe place for valuables, because he didn't *have* valuables. The silver pen was the first and only thing anyone would want to steal from him. And it wasn't only that Ned wouldn't want to explain to Crispin that he'd let it get half-inched; he couldn't risk the consequences. He'd seen what happened to the fellow who wrote with old Marleigh's haunted pen. No thief or fence deserved that.

So to stop Crispin carrying the pen around in his pocket, Ned was carrying it around in his own. He wasn't sure if he liked this turn of events.

Crispin. It had been a week and a half since poor silent Voake had burned in his own shop, and it didn't look like they were nearer finding out why. Crispin had done his best, Ned knew; he'd spent half a day helping Janossi look through what sounded like a right shambles of an office to find a lost picture, for whatever peculiar reason. He'd got himself on the man's right side and done his best to find out more. It had come to nothing, but that wasn't Crispin's fault.

Probably. Not that Ned doubted him, he knew Crispin would have given it a good shot, but there was no denying he was focused on his own studies. This Dr. Sweet of his… Well, Ned was glad for him, he truly was. He was glad that Crispin had a teacher who saw what Ned did: the stubborn heart, the sharp mind, the man who deserved a chance. The talent. He'd seen Crispin three times since he'd started studying with Dr. Sweet, and each time he'd been glowing more, with pride in his own achievements and in his teacher's satisfaction with his progress. Sweet thought Crispin was valuable. Special. Precious.

So did Ned, but nobody asked him. He'd told Crispin a dozen times to have faith in himself, to believe he was as worthy as anyone. Seemed like it was more convincing coming from a magician than a waste-man.

He was *not* going to whine about this. If Crispin found his place and his self-confidence, that was good, and if that meant him going off into his own world of strange studies and unthinkable powers and leaving Ned behind, that was the way of things. They'd had fun, and he didn't propose to taint it with resentment, or do anything to spoil things for Crispin when they were starting to go right at last. That wasn't what you'd do if you cared for a fellow. Not if you really cared.

He'd been fine before Crispin turned up in his paper store sweaty and panicking; he'd be fine when he drifted away again. In the meantime he'd enjoy what they had and not spoil it with stupid thinking and wanting and nonsense just because Crispin was, in the end, going to want more out of his exciting, magical, privileged, educated, *white* world than a dusty waste-man in shabby clothes living round the back of a closed-up rag and bottle.

He exhaled hard, and someone said, "Goodness. Don't blow all the leaves off."

Ned looked round, startled. He hadn't noticed anyone joining him, but there he was, a young chap with a jagged streak of white running through his black hair, like a lightning strike. He was good-looking, blue-eyed, smartly dressed with a flash blue waistcoat, and if ever Ned had seen *untrustworthy*, it was sitting on the bench next to him.

"I won't do that if you keep your hands out of my pockets," Ned said pleasantly. "And if this is a confidence game, let's say I got none and leave it at that."

The blue-eyed man gave a startled snort of laughter. "You're blunt."

Ned shrugged. Blue Eyes made a face. "I'm quite sure I could persuade you that I'm an entirely inoffensive fellow wanting a chat, but actually, you've saved me a bit of trouble working up to this: What *is* it that you have in your inside left jacket pocket? Pure curiosity," he added, as Ned straightened threateningly. "I wouldn't touch it, frankly."

"Who says I've got anything in my pocket?"

Blue Eyes gave a sudden wide, absurdly charming smile. "You've checked it's there three times since you sat down. Yes, I was watching. But, not to put too fine a point on it, you are aware that what you're carrying isn't…usual?"

"Ah," Ned said. "You're one of *them*, are you?"

"I am 'one of them' in every possible sense of 'them'," his companion agreed cheerfully. "And what you're carrying reeks of power, and since it's clear you *aren't* 'one of them', which is to say 'us', and I'm only killing time anyway, I thought I'd ask what on earth you were doing and if you actually knew what you were about."

"Right, got you," Ned said. "And the answer is, none of your business."

"Spoilsport." The young man leaned back. "Lovely day, isn't it?"

Ned shot him an unfriendly look and, since he'd already given himself away like a right green 'un, checked that the pen was actually still in his pocket. It was. "How can you tell?" he asked.

"Look at the sky. Oh, tell about what you're carrying?" Blue Eyes shrugged. "It's in the wind."

"Mph. Here, do you know anything about spontaneous combustion?"

Blue Eyes considered that. "Do you know, that might be the most peculiar question I've ever been asked while sitting on a park bench. No, I don't. I believe there was a case in London a good few years ago—"

"A rag'n'bottler. I heard."

"Well, that's all I know. Why?"

"Just asking."

"As one does," Blue Eyes batted back.

"Right, well. But if a fellow had died of that here, you reckon you'd see something *in the wind*?"

"I can't imagine I wouldn't. Is there any way I can persuade you to tell me why you're asking?"

He wasn't justiciary, that was obvious. The very opposite, in fact. Ned could see no harm in trying to get some information. "Say a fellow burned to death that way. And say there was strange noises, *and* one of your lot had done some magic in there on top of it all. Why would a justiciar say there'd been nothing magic gone on?"

"Probably because they're smug, self-righteous bastards who aren't nearly as clever as they think they are," Blue Eyes said with feeling. "If you've got mixed up with them, I'm sorry for you. But to answer your question... Well, magic leaves traces in the ether. That's how it works. So either the justiciar is lying, or he's horribly incompetent, or whoever did the burning is very good at covering their traces." He frowned a little. "I'd wonder about that."

"How's that?"

"Well, if I wanted to commit a murder that didn't come to the attention of the justiciary, I'd probably use a knife." The young man spoke with a mild technical interest that made the hairs rise on Ned's neck. "It would be a great deal less effort than setting someone on fire, for me at least. Killing people in wildly dramatic ways is almost guaranteed to get the justiciary's attention, which tends to end poorly. So covering your tracks is a marvellous idea, but it makes a great deal more sense to avoid their notice in the first place." He made a face, then pulled out what looked to Ned's eye like a staggeringly expensive gold fob watch. "On that note, I must go, I have someone to meet. Good luck with whatever it is you're up to, and thank you for being such a charming way to kill time." He gave a flashing grin. "I'm quite nervous, you see, and I like to talk when I'm nervous."

"Yeah, you look terrified," Ned said drily. "Good luck to you too, mate."

Blue Eyes sauntered off. Ned checked that he hadn't spirited away the pen as he went—wouldn't put anything past a chap with a face like that—and sat back to consider.

He'd no reason to trust Blue Eyes, but on the other hand, the fellow hadn't had a reason to lie. And he had made a good point. If you wanted Voake dead, what was wrong with a blackjack to the skull, or even a muffler over his face while he slept off a bottle of gin? Why would you kill a man in such a theatrical way and then go to the effort of covering all traces?

Voake had, far as Ned could tell, no relatives, no goods to leave, no enemies. The shop was shuttered; if anyone was planning to come take it over, they hadn't told Ned about it. So why kill him?

All right, think it out: Either he'd been murdered on purpose, and it was impossible to see how Voake could've made that kind of enemy. Or he'd been killed unintentionally, and whoever did it had covered their traces magically after. That was plausible on the face of it, but could you set a man on fire by accident? Or Janossi had been lying, but there was Crispin making friends with him and not reporting any trouble…

It didn't make sense. Something, as far as Ned understood it, had wiped the air clean of magical traces, while leaving the physical evidence of crime behind.

It made sense if a magician had really wanted to kill Voake and had absolutely no other way to do it except setting him on fire. That would explain things all right, except for why would you want to and why you couldn't find a better way, so it was no explanation at all, really. At least it fitted the facts better than saying maybe rag'n'bottlers just caught fire now and again.

Ha. For all he knew there was some balmy magician setting fire to rag'n'bottlers all over London and everyone was saying, ooh, well, there was a fellow thirty years ago…

Ned thought about that. Then he stood, took up his cart, and set off eastwards. It was the direction of home but there was, he recalled, a rag and bottle on Denmark Place, on the other side of Charing Cross Road. He might as well stop over there on the way.

In the end, he stopped at them all.

It was stupid. He wasn't a peeler or a practitioner, let alone a justiciar. But no other so-and-so was looking, and Voake had died a bad death, and mostly, it had been Ned alone at the pauper's funeral, burying cinders in a child-size coffin made out of wood that was barely thicker than paper. Crispin had been busy with Dr. Sweet, like he always was these days, and there had been nobody else at all to come. No wife, no family, nobody but the waste-man next door.

Ned didn't have family himself, not since he'd been caught kissing a sailor. His brother had put the boot in, and then his father had used his fists, and then he'd heard the church was going to pray for him and he'd got out of Shad Thames faster than a scalded cat. Having his business announced to the whole congregation didn't sound like a good plan if he wanted to make it to the following Sunday. So no family, and most like no wife or children to come, and maybe he'd die an old man with another old fellow by his side, but he wouldn't want to bet on it. That wasn't how things were. He'd go into the ground in a cheap coffin and hope his neighbours came to see him off, just as he would them till that day, because that was the right thing to do.

And if some bloody awful thing happened to push him off the mortal coil, he'd like to think that someone, somewhere would care.

So Ned set his shoulders, already aching with lugging the cart, and trudged the long way home by way of every damn rag and bottle he could think of.

No, they all said. *Fires? Not heard anything like that. No, we're all very well. Jug with a bearded face? No such thing here.* He looped through and back the mess of little roads that was Seven Dials, four, five, six shops, all blank faces and incomprehension, until he blew out a breath and pushed open the door of a rag and bottle on Great Earl Street.

"Excuse me, missus, sorry to bother you. Bit of a funny question, but I'm looking to find out about a rag'n'bottler who's come to harm recently—"

"George Reed, you mean?"

"Could be," Ned said. "Could rightly be. Can you tell me about that?"

She was, she said, too busy. Ned doubted that, with the shop empty and her eyes flicking about like she was looking to call for help. But she willingly directed him to Reed's shop, all the way down Bedfordbury. He heard the door give a resounding slam after him as he left.

Ned heaved his way south, making a mental note that this was the last stop; he'd keep looking tomorrow, but his boots were like to wear out this way, if not his feet first. He also made mental notes on his opinion of magicians in general and Mr. Janossi in particular, on rag'n'bottlers and their stupid habits of dying, and on what he'd have to do to get a new handcart because if he had to listen to that bloody squeaky axle much more he'd land in Colney Hatch. He had more or less persuaded himself that his entire afternoon had been nothing but a waste of time when he arrived at the rag and bottle he'd been sent to find.

It was closed up. Ned knocked a bit, then a bit more, and he was considering which neighbours would be best approached when he saw a stir of movement through the window, and the door opened.

The woman who peered out was heavy-eyed and dressed in black, so he took a guess. "Mrs. Reed?"

"And who might you be?"

"Name's Ned Hall. I'm sorry to intrude at a time of grief, but could you spare me a minute?"

"About what?"

Ned took a gamble. "A rag'n'bottler, a friend of mine, died recently. In an odd sort of way. Very odd. I'm wanting to know more."

Mrs. Reed looked at him for a second longer, then opened the door fully. "I'd say you'd better come in."

She invited him to sit, which was a relief, and made tea. Ned glanced around while she did it, looking for scorch marks, saw nothing.

"Well." She handed him the mug. "You want to know about my husband's passing, is that it?"

"If you don't mind."

Her throat convulsed. "We'd been married thirty-six years last Christmas, me and my George, and he's dead. Yes, I *mind*. You said an odd death. How odd?"

"Very."

"Yes, well." She stared at her work-thickened fingers around the mug. "I'll tell you what I know, which is what I told the crowner and the peelers, for all the good it's done. We went to bed like usual, a little over a week ago. When I woke in the morning, he wasn't there. I come downstairs to start the fire, and there he is on the shop floor, dead as a doornail, with his mouth stuffed full of mud."

"Mud?" Ned said blankly.

"That's right. In his mouth and in his poor throat and the crowner said he'd breathed it into his lungs—he always had a bad chest—I was knitting him a scarf—"

She squeezed her eyes shut. Ned grimaced. "I'm so sorry, missus. But, do you know—"

"How? No, I don't. They said, no sign of a struggle. They said—do you know what they said? They said he must have eaten it. Choked himself to death on dirt! No other explanation, that's what they said!" Her voice was rising and cracking with indignation. "They reckon my George came downstairs and sat in the shop and shovelled dirt into his mouth till he suffocated himself on it!"

"With what?" Ned asked. "I mean, sorry to say it, missus, but where'd the earth come from? Did he have a box of it, or—"

"No," she said fiercely. "Nor anything like. Nothing at all. As if he'd gone outside and eaten himself stuffed on muck and come back in and locked the door behind him and lain down to die."

Ned tried to picture it. "There was no struggle, and the doors were locked?"

"Locked and bolted. So it can't have been murder done, that's what they're saying. They'd rather say my George was mad as Nebuchadnezzar, eating grass." She put her barely touched mug down. "So what do you know, Mr. Hall?"

"I don't know what I know," Ned said. "Mr. Voake, had the rag and bottle up Grape Street? He's dead too, but not like this. He burned. In his shop, but it was him burning, not the shop on fire, if you understand me. Locked doors, middle of the night. Uh, how long ago did Mr. Reed pass on?"

"It happened on the night of the twentieth."

"Twentieth," Ned repeated. "Right. Well. There's a coincidence."

Mrs. Reed looked at him with dawning horror. "God save us."

"Hope so," Ned said. "Missus, this is going to seem a fool's question, but I've a reason for it. You don't have on the premises such a thing as a Bellarmine or Bartmann jug? Earthenware or stoneware, like a bottle with a handle and a bearded face on it?"

"On the premises? No, I can't say I do," she said. "We only ever had the one and I sold that Monday."

"You had one? You had a jug like that? When Mr. Reed—"

"It was right there in the shop." She looked at him with a kind of unfocused fear. "What's wrong? Should I not have sold it?"

"I've no idea," Ned said. "But there's no *should* and you've nothing to reproach yourself for, I'm sure of that. Any idea who you sold it to?"

The widow opened her mouth, and stopped with a frown. After a moment she shook her head. "I can't place it. I know I had one, and sold it. It was to…to a… I can't think. Why can't I think? It's like a fog. I sold it to—to—" She made a frustrated gesture.

Crispin could bring memories back; he'd done it to Ned. Ned thought that, and the next thought came on its heels: If magicians could summon up memories, could they cloud them?

He needed to talk to Crispin right now. Problem was, he wasn't like to see him till tomorrow evening.

He bade Mrs. Reed farewell, assuring her he'd let her know what he found out, and headed back towards Grape Street, hauling the handcart over bumpy cobbles and high kerbs, with something in his gut that, after a while, he realised was anger.

How dare some blasted abracadabra merchant make that woman a widow? How dare they bring foul, lonely deaths to Voake and Reed, and leave a woman alone in her old age, and tamper with her mind as well? How dare they take Crispin as the pretty-fey, bullied boy he'd been, and twist his talents, and then condemn him for what he'd been made, and *then* he still wanted to be part of their damn secret society where Ned wouldn't ever be? How dare the bastards do any of it?

He bloody hated magicians.

CHAPTER SIX

"Write me light," said Dr. Sweet.

Crispin closed his fingers on the pen, controlling his breathing. It was a plain, normal fountain pen, because it wasn't the silver pen that did it; he didn't need to use blood and bone. He was a graphomancer. His powers came into play at the point where the ether met the material world, where the nib met the paper and the ink trapped meaning.

He sketched the litterae, the symbols that, he'd been taught, gave his writing its power. Dr. Sweet said he would be able to drop them one day, but for now, they gave him confidence. They were something familiar, reminding him of the snakebite of his real—his *old* pen as it sucked strength from his own blood. It had hurt, but it was easy. This was hard.

Hard, but possible.

Here we go…

Crispin's focus shrunk to the nib as it hovered over the paper. He could feel the potential around him, the channel waiting to be lit up.

He wrote *Lux*, and as he wrote he felt it, in his fingertips and down his spine. He felt his skin tingle and he felt the ether quiver in response, and before his stunned, joyful gaze, light bloomed in the air like an unfurling flower.

Not his witchlight. He'd *written* it. And—

"Dr. Sweet," he said urgently. "Dr. Sweet!"

"Tell me." Dr. Sweet was smiling.

"Resonance." Crispin shook with the combination of power and excitement. "What Mr. Maupert was trying to teach me—I can feel it in my hand! In the writing!"

"Can you indeed?" Dr. Sweet's expression of satisfaction was a reward in itself. "You've made the connection. Very good. *Very* good."

Crispin's pen hissed over the paper, a swooping line that changed the light in the room to red. He didn't *have* to see the ether, or hear it, or smell it as others did. Those weren't his senses; this was. He wrote a flourish across the page and felt the meaning echo back at him from all around.

"Glorious. *Glorious*, Crispin."

Crispin lifted his pen, letting the light die. "Oh God, I can do it. It's wonderful. It's…I can feel it. I can write it, ink on a page, and it *happens*."

"Precisely. Your act is amplified in the world. As above, so below." Dr. Sweet raised a brow at what must have been Crispin's blank expression. "You aren't familiar with that? It's from the *Hermetica*, the writings of the great occultist Hermes Trismegistus. I'd have thought Marleigh would have taught you Trismegistus."

"No, I've never read it." Crispin knew the name, though. "Uh, I wasn't aware that was approved of?"

"Well, it's certainly not a regular textbook," Dr. Sweet admitted. "But then, you don't have regular talents. We don't all operate within the same constraints, you know, and some of the old ways have a great deal to teach us." He had moved to a bookcase as he spoke, and now he took down an old, leather-bound volume. "Listen. 'That which is above is the same as that which is below, and that which is below is the same as that which is above, for the performance of miracles of the

One Thing. And as all things are from the One, by the meditation of One, so all things have their birth from this One Thing by adaptation. The Sun is its Father, the Moon its Mother, the Wind carries it in its belly, its nurse is the Earth. This is the Father of all perfection, or consummation of the whole world.'"

"Um," Crispin said. He had a sudden picture of what Ned's expression would be if he read that out, and had to hold in a hiccup of laughter.

"Yes, it is a little obscure." Dr. Sweet's eyes twinkled. "But the principle is important. As above, so below. The world is the same as man, and man is the same as the smallest cell in his body. The poet Blake, a great if eccentric practitioner, says 'To see the world in a grain of sand, and heaven in a wild flower, hold Infinity in the palm of your hand and Eternity in an hour.' Your act of writing resonates through the ether and the world. It's merely a question of making the connection."

Crispin nodded. He felt awestruck and tingly, light-headed with a huge, joyful sense of possibility, and also very hungry. Dr. Sweet beamed. "An excellent afternoon's work. I shall see you tomorrow. Practice, my boy, and make sure you take some time to be proud of yourself."

Crispin found himself grinning so widely that his face hurt. "I will. I can't thank you enough."

"Nonsense, it's my privilege. And that brings me to something else: at some point, you will need to stand before the Council and demonstrate that your talents have nothing to do with warlockry. I should like to see you do that before I leave—"

"Leave?" Crispin said, with a plunging sensation.

"Well, my dear chap, I'm only here for a short time. I came to pursue my own researches, you know."

Crispin felt a pang of guilt. He'd known Dr. Sweet had other work, but he'd not so much as asked, let alone wondered if the man really had time for the intensive teaching he was giving. "Yes, of course. I hope that's going well?"

"Oh, tolerably, thank you. I'm perhaps halfway to success."

He'd been here less than a fortnight. Did that mean he'd be gone in the same length of time? Crispin's anxiety doubtless showed, because Dr. Sweet patted his shoulder. "Don't worry. As secondary projects go, you are the most fascinating one I could have hoped for. In fact, I meant to ask, and now seems as good a time as any. Is there anything tying you to London in particular? That's a Cornish accent, is it not?"

"How do you mean, tying me?"

"Well, I rather wondered if you'd consider coming to Oxford with me," Dr. Sweet said calmly. "I'm fascinated by your gift, and the more I see of it, the more applications I can see for my own work. I study the old forms, you know, the old ways, which are so much more tactile and tangible than modern theory. I should very much like to see if we could work together."

Crispin's mouth was hanging open, he realised. "I...I mean..."

"No need to decide at once. It is a large commitment, and we would have a great deal to discuss first. But as a possibility—"

"It would be marvellous," Crispin said on a breath.

He considered it, heading down the stairs. To work with Dr. Sweet, whose calm patience had done more in a handful of days than seven months with London's busy, irritable teachers. To be treated as a rare talent, a useful one. To be wanted.

To be in the country again. Oxford was a city, but a small provincial one. He could walk out into the countryside in an hour, he could be out of the stink and smoke and the press of people and the awfulness of everyone knowing his past...

Away from Ned.

He could still see him. It would mean Crispin coming back to London, of course. Ned couldn't afford days without earnings, or railway tickets. And though Crispin had never been to Oxford, he was fairly sure you wouldn't get many men of colour there, and those you did would be students or academics, not paper-dusty labourers. Ned would be looked at. Which was risky for them as a pair, but Crispin also knew he didn't like it. They'd walked down the river once on a Sunday, and a couple of children with their nursemaid had come up to Ned and asked if they could touch him to see what his skin felt like. He had turned it off with a laugh and a pleasant word, but Crispin didn't think he'd really found it amusing at all.

No, Ned probably wouldn't go to Oxford. But Crispin could come back here. Once a month, perhaps, for a couple of days at a time. People did worse. Women waited at home for years for their men gone overseas.

Crispin wondered if Ned would wait, and for how long.

He couldn't turn down a chance like this. That would be stupid beyond belief. Ned wouldn't expect that, surely?

Well, no, he wouldn't, because he'd think of what was best for Crispin and what was common sense. He wouldn't say, *No, don't go, I don't care what he's offering you, I want you with me forever*—or words to that effect, because Crispin couldn't imagine him saying anything of the kind.

He wished to hell that Ned would.

It was absurd. If he wanted grand emotional gestures and passion, he was with the wrong man. Ned was all calm good sense and steady strength, and doing the right thing because it needed doing. He coped with things, kept his feet on the ground, didn't make a fuss or get upset. Crispin had seen him angry, but never for long. He couldn't imagine him crying.

Ned was everything Crispin wanted to be, and a fair portion of everything he wanted, right here in London. But everything else he wanted was being offered to him in Oxford. And now he had no idea at all what to do.

He headed for the door to the corridor that led to the justiciary offices. He'd found the paper Janossi had been looking for the previous week; it was a picture of a serious-looking man that had been drawn by the murderous painter last winter. Janossi had needed it for an investigation, but he'd promised that Crispin could have it to examine when they were done, so he might as well pick it up.

He turned into the justiciary corridor and found himself face to face, or chest to face given the man's stature, with the senior justiciar Stephen Day. Mr. Day shot him a look suggesting that Crispin should be the one to move. He was escorting the miserable-looking man Crispin had seen hanging around a while back—who was, he realised, the subject of the painter's soul-trapping portrait. No wonder he looked so unhappy. Crispin couldn't forbear offering a sympathetic smile as he skipped out of the way. The man didn't appear to notice.

The corridor was deserted once they'd gone. Crispin headed for Janossi's study, which he'd helped put into some semblance of order. You could call it currying favour, because it was, but under the circumstances, making someone in the justiciary like him had seemed a good idea.

If he went to Oxford, he wouldn't need to do that.

The portrait was on Janossi's desk, with a note saying, *CT— Yours!* Interpreting that as permission, Crispin picked it up and ran his fingers carefully over the pencilled lines of the face, the strong jaw and serious eyes. It felt dead, somehow, which boded ill for its unhappy subject until he realised he must be sensing the artist's death. Still, tracing the lines, he could feel the etheric connections stirring like cobwebs shaking in a breeze, the shadows of power. He could tell how the painter had done his work, woven the skein around and into his victim. Not that Crispin would do something like that, but he could feel the possibility...

"What the hell are you doing?"

Crispin jumped about a foot. Waterford stood glaring at him in the doorway.

"What's it to you?" he demanded, trying not to sound upset at the shock.

Waterford strode forward, batting down the paper in Crispin's hand to get a good look at it. This close, Crispin could hear the air whistle through his squashed nose as he breathed. "Ha! I knew it. Practising, are you? Who are you going to draw?" He snatched at the paper. Crispin jerked it away just in time. "I'll make sure the Yid knows about this."

"You are so rude," Crispin made himself say. There were a few practitioners who spoke disrespectfully of Dr. and Mrs. Gold's religion—although never, he noticed, to their faces or when any of the justiciary might hear—and it gave him the same squirmy feeling of wrongness that he felt at the looks Ned sometimes got. He always thought he ought to say something. This was the first time he had. "And *actually*, Janossi said I could have this for study, as if it's any of your business what I do."

"A warlock sneaking around the justiciary offices while they're empty?" Waterford said scathingly.

"I'm not sneaking. Anyway, what are *you* doing here? Your master was plotting against the justiciary, wasn't he? Using this." He waved the picture, keeping it well out of Waterford's reach. "Were you hoping to get your hands on it? Finish his work?"

It was a completely baseless accusation, pulled out of the air in an effort not to be on the back foot. People said the best defence was a good offence. Crispin wasn't one to go on the offensive as a rule, but he had Dr. Sweet's words in his ears still, and he was sick of Waterford's spite.

He didn't expect the man to turn white with shock.

"Rubbish." Waterford's nasal voice trembled slightly. "What he did wasn't anything to do with me. It wasn't my fault—"

"Didn't you try to get Saint into trouble for him?" Crispin demanded, pressing his advantage with a heady sense of power. "Isn't that why she spoiled your face?"

Waterford's hand came up over his destroyed nose, an obviously involuntary movement. "Go to hell," he said, voice thick, and turned on his heel.

Crispin stared after him as he hurried away. His heart was thumping, as it always did with confrontation, and he felt slightly quivery, but he'd stood up for himself. He really had, for once, stood up for himself against Waterford's bullying, and the man would probably think twice about insulting him again. He folded the paper away with a shaky hand, taking his time because he didn't want to push his luck by encountering Waterford in the corridors again. He'd probably be angry.

He hadn't *looked* angry.

He'd looked utterly miserable. He'd looked very like Crispin felt when he heard *warlock* muttered or spat, and it suddenly occurred to him that he might not be the first person to have said that. Waterford's master had helped murder police officers and caused any amount of trouble that was still bitterly resented, and Crispin had been one of the fascinated onlookers when Mr. Day and Mrs. Gold had stormed into the Council, brandishing the man's severed head.

Crispin had loved Mr. Marleigh, and part of him still did, even knowing that he'd been a murderer and a liar and not Mr. Marleigh at all. He wondered if Waterford had loved his own treacherous master, and how it had felt to see him *decapitated*, for God's sake, let alone what it was like to have that awful lump of a nose disfiguring his face.

The sense of achievement at his victory wisped away as though it had never been. He hadn't triumphed over Waterford, he'd just bullied him back. And won, and maybe that was something, but it didn't feel like much.

I don't want to win, Crispin thought. *If these are the rules of the game, I don't want to win, I don't even want to play.*

What he wanted, suddenly and urgently, was Ned.

When he came round to the paper store's back door, it was unlocked. He knocked anyway and heard Ned's grunt.

He was sitting on a stack of waste, back to the wall, knees to his chest, which didn't look like an easy position for a man of his muscles, holding his battered hip flask in a loose manner that suggested it was empty.

"Are you all right?" Crispin asked in lieu of greeting. Ned wasn't teetotal but he wasn't a drinker either, and that combined with his posture was rather unnerving. "Ned?"

Ned grunted again, then tipped his head back to rest against the dusty wall. "Not so chipper, no."

Crispin bolted the door and came to sit beside him. "What's wrong?"

Ned tapped the cheap tin flask against his leg, a little irritable movement. "I don't know. You tell me."

"Um…" Crispin had an absurd surge of guilt, as if Ned could have found out about the Oxford offer already, and shoved it back. "I'm not sure what you mean."

"Tell you, then. My pal Voake gets burned to death, with a Bellarmine jug singing along. Funny thing is, the same night, another rag'n'bottler dies. Chokes on earth on the floor of his shop, middle of the night, and he's supposed to have eaten it but there's no bowl and spoon, and the doors are locked, and you know what he had on his shelf? A Bellarmine jug."

"*What?*"

"Which," Ned went on inexorably, "a bit later someone comes and buys, and the funny thing is, the widow can't remember anything about who bought it. Not a thing. Remembers the other sales, remembers she had one, but this fellow, or it might have been a lady for all she knows, the memory's gone. Which—"

"Fluence," Crispin said. "It's a magical way of influencing people's minds."

"Thought so." Ned's jaw hardened. "So what is this, then? Two dead, two Bellarmine jugs—"

"But isn't the one next door still there? And if someone wanted to collect them, couldn't they have bought them in the usual way?"

"I don't know. Because I don't know anything about this bloody Godless business of yours. I don't like it."

"You don't like this business with the jugs?" Crispin said hopefully.

"I don't like magic. That's what it comes down to. This ain't right. What good's it do? All these people with powers, what good are you doing with 'em?"

"I—but— Well, what do you want done?" Crispin asked. "I'd like to not do any harm, for a start."

"Yeah, that's it. You work your hardest and you might not raise any corpses or ruin some poor woman's life."

"Oh, come on! That's not fair."

"Nor's what happened to Voake, nor Reed, the other chap." Ned looked round at him at last. His face, normally so relaxed, was twisted. "I talked to the widow, you know? Which is more than any of your lot did—"

"They might not even have known. I'll ask Janossi—"

"Because he was so much use with Voake?"

"I'm not sure what else I can do," Crispin said, stuttering a bit because he had an awful feeling growing in his stomach. "I don't know what you want me to say."

Ned banged the back of his head against the wall, sending off-white dust puffing over his tight-curled hair. "I want to feel like someone cares. I want to know anyone except me gives a monkey's that there's two men died foul, lonely deaths and a widow left alone. You know how I found out about Reed? I went and asked at a lot of rag and bottles, that's all. Wasn't hard. But nobody else has."

"I was—" Crispin stopped himself, too late.

"Busy? Course. You were too busy for Voake's funeral too."

"I barely knew him!"

"I did," Ned said. "Lived next door to him for years. I'd have liked to see him sent off decent, not just me there. The parson might have made a bit of an effort if there'd been more than one man watching."

He should have gone, Crispin knew that. He made a face. "You're right. I'm sorry."

"Me too." Ned blew out a long, hard breath. "Two dead, and nobody else cares. None of your lot do, that's clear enough, and the peelers certainly don't. Well, I do, that's all. Maybe I've been too long a waste-man, but I don't like to see anything thrown away."

Crispin put a very tentative hand on his knee. "I understand. Um, I know I've not been around much, but if you want me to help—"

"Not sure what you'd do. I'm not a peeler or a magician, how should I know?" He slapped the flask rhythmically against his knee. "I found out about Reed yesterday afternoon. Spent today going round every rag and bottle I could find, maybe thirty of 'em. I thought I'd see if there was any other strange dead while I was at it, or any other of these damn jugs. Short of visiting everyone in London, I don't know what else to do."

"Was there anything else?"

"Well, there was a rag'n'bottler's wife found dead on the floor last week. Paternoster Street. That got my attention. Been suffocated, the neighbours said. Husband's been arrested for murder. He's saying he never did it, but he would, wouldn't he." Ned shrugged. "Might be nothing. It was a week after Voake died. I asked if they had a Bellarmine jug in the shop anyway."

"Did they?"

"Dunno. Bloke told me to piss off or he'd set the dogs on me."

"Oh Lord." Crispin squeezed his knee. "I'm sorry." He searched for something helpful to say. "Look, I really will bring the other death to the justiciary's attention. I am quite sure they'll follow that up. And…I could ask Dr. Sweet."

"What good'll that do?"

"I don't know if it'll be any but he's an antiquarian, he studies the old forms of magic. I bet he knows about witch bottles. He might know something about Bellarmine jugs—*and* I could explain to him about the fire, and why Janossi was wrong about the traces in the ether— God, I should have thought of that before."

"Yeah," Ned said, staring at him. "Sounds like you should."

Crispin groped for an excuse. "Well, but I… Everything was all happening at once, and I was thinking about my studies—"

"Like usual."

"Well, what am I supposed to do?" Crispin pulled his hand away. "I can't stop being a magician, and I have actually been in quite a lot of trouble these last months. Now I have a chance to learn how to do things properly and make something of myself, and I'm going to take it."

"Course you are."

"Well, I am! And I'm sorry if you don't like it."

"Not up to me, is it?"

"No, actually, it's not." Crispin wasn't quite sure if he was standing up for himself or losing his temper. Both feelings were unfamiliar. "I don't tell you how to run your business—"

"I don't need telling," Ned said. "It's not like it's complicated, is it, hauling paper around and dickering over the price? Not like *magic*." There was an unfamiliar note of bitter irony in his voice. Crispin wasn't sure why, and he felt too hurt and angry to ask. He couldn't help it if he wasn't the man Ned was, able to do a day's hard physical work and live by his own sweat and wit. He knew perfectly well he couldn't make a living on London's streets, or a living at all from his bizarre, specialised, borderline-useless talents.

He couldn't help being less than Ned, he hated it, and he didn't like to have it rubbed in his face.

"Well, I'm sorry to have bothered you with it," he snapped. "But it *is* important to me, and if you think I should make myself useful then maybe you shouldn't complain when I try to do exactly that. When I have my powers under control—"

"You'll go off and be the Grand Panjandrum somewhere, leave the little folk behind."

"Well, maybe I will!" Crispin could feel his cheeks burning. "Because, actually, Dr. Sweet's asked me to go and study with him in Oxford. At All Souls College. *He* thinks my talents are worth cultivating." Which was, apparently, more than Ned did. It hurt immensely.

Ned's mouth opened a little, with a look of something like shock. "Oxford," he repeated. "You're going to Oxford."

"I could *do* something with my talent, you know." Maybe he wasn't practical, or strong, or cunning, but by God he could be *something*, he could become the calm, competent professional he never felt. "I could make something of myself."

"Right." Ned's cheeks were darker than usual. "And never mind about the widow woman and poor bloody burned Voake."

"I said I'd help with that!"

"When you thought of it." Ned shook his head. "Look, I know the magic's important to you, it's your job. I didn't reckon it had to be your whole life, or that it had to be more important than other people's lives, but if I was wrong about that, well, that's down to you. Not my business. But…there's plenty of people ready to tell me my place." He made a gesture encompassing his dust, his worn, cheap clothing. "And I don't need that in my home, and I don't need you doing it at all."

"What? I didn't—"

"Yeah, you do, and I'm not in the mood." Ned stood. "I might not be worth much out there, but I don't have to be second best in here. Off you hop."

"Excuse me?" Crispin said blankly. "What do you mean, second best?"

"Look," Ned said. "I'm pissed off. I've been pissed off for a while, and I'm not less pissed off after this conversation. So we can have a great big billingsgate, you and me, and both say a lot of things we won't forget in a hurry, or you can clear off till we both calm down and maybe we'll part on good terms—"

"Part," Crispin repeated, with a dreadful sucking plunge like a sinkhole opening in his gut.

"What else would you call it if you're off to the university? Go on, Crispin. Take a walk." He sounded very weary. "I've been on my feet all day and I'm too tired for this."

"Right," Crispin said. "Fine. I, uh—fine. I'll go then."

"You do that."

Crispin rose. Headed for the door without kissing Ned goodbye. Left without looking round and heard the door bolted behind him, and set off down Grape Street, staring at the cobbles through a distorting film of tears.

Everything was awful and he'd done it all wrong, and he wasn't even quite sure how that argument had happened. He'd wanted to talk to Ned, to discuss the whole Oxford problem properly…

But tonight Ned had needed someone to talk to, and Crispin hadn't done that very well.

He walked home alone, with a lump in his throat that felt the size and spikiness of a horse-chestnut shell.

He did talk to Dr. Sweet the next day, because even if Ned was sick of him, which apparently he was, he should see that Crispin kept his promises.

He spilled it all out after the lesson. Nearly all, anyway, because he didn't want to be asked too closely about why he'd been there in the middle of the night, so he…reshaped the story a little. He'd been having a late drink with his friend Hall, that was all, when the singing had come.

"This man could hear it?" Dr. Sweet asked.

"He's a flit." Crispin winced slightly as he said it. It was such a dismissive word. *I might not be worth much out there…*

Dr. Sweet nodded. Crispin carried on: the burning man, the pen, the lack of trace of anything in the ether afterwards, and Ned's discovery of the second death.

"Good Lord," Dr. Sweet said at the end of his recital. "That's quite a tale. Have you taken it to the justiciary?"

"Not since I called Janossi in. I couldn't say about the pen, you see." Dr. Sweet's understanding look made Crispin, perversely, flush with shame. "I should have told him, I know, but I didn't. So he didn't really want to listen after that. And then Ned—Hall—only told me the rest yesterday."

"He sounds a determined man, this Mr. Hall."

"He is. He's determined, and he's good at doing things, and he cares about people." The words ached. "He won't rest until he's found out what happened to Voake."

"Praiseworthy." Dr. Sweet frowned. "But perhaps also risky. Is he working with anyone? The police?"

"No," Crispin said, with a twinge of pride. "He's found out everything himself. Well, nearly," honesty compelled him to add. "He found a woman rag'n'bottler who died as well, but he couldn't find if she had a Bellarmine jug in the shop. I'm going to check that today."

"Do you know," Dr. Sweet said slowly, "if you'd permit it, I'd rather you let me do that. I might be able to, uh, help your witnesses recover any clouded memories you see."

"Oh! Really?"

"Well, I must admit I'd rather you didn't take this tale of using your pen to the justiciary." Dr. Sweet gave him a rueful look. "Since I'm vouching for your reformation. And after all, it might be nothing.

Your friend sounds a dedicated man, but even dedicated men get bees in their bonnets. I'll tell you what we'll do. I shall go to your friend, get his story, and have a jolly good look at this Bellarmine jug. Then I'll go to the various shops and see if I can find any residual traces of misapplied power. If it seems as though something criminal is going on, you and I will present our case to the justiciary together, and I think they will not ignore me quite so easily as all that."

Crispin was glad he was sitting down: his knees felt weak. "That would be wonderful. I really can't thank you enough, Doctor."

"On the contrary, my boy, it is I who am I obliged to you."

"Why?" Crispin asked blankly.

Dr. Sweet's eyes twinkled. "Well, you make my life so much more interesting."

CHAPTER SEVEN

Crispin spent the rest of the day in Dr. Sweet's study, practising. Dr. Sweet hadn't been able to start on his investigation at once because of a string of appointments, but he had taken down Ned's address and assured Crispin he would begin the next day. Meanwhile, and rather less pleasingly, he'd asked Crispin to stay well away from every rag and bottle shop in London, which meant not visiting Ned.

"You have ill-wishers," he'd said frankly. "I can imagine how your crossing my trail, as it were, might be misinterpreted. No, please keep your distance, for my peace of mind, until I report back to you."

Crispin had agreed with some reluctance, against his urge to rush over to Grape Street and tell Ned, *See, I have done something*. Perhaps it would be better to wait anyway. It would be quite the coup to present Ned with a complete answer to the puzzle. Show him there was something useful magic could do.

So he settled to work as best he could, concentrating fiercely, although the commotion that erupted in the late afternoon did bring him out to discover what in the world was going on. He came downstairs, and stuck his head into the main hall to see Mrs. Gold and the Councillor Mrs. Baron Shaw in frantic and loud conversation. Mrs. Baron Shaw looked harassed. Mrs. Gold looked enormous.

"It was that blasted windwalker." Mrs. Gold propped her hands where her hips ought to have been. "We took the prisoner Spenser to Cannon Street nick to try and draw that airborne pestilence Pastern out of hiding. That succeeded magnificently, right up to the point he arrived, after which things fell apart somewhat. He plucked Spenser out of our hands, and the pair of them got clean away. And in the course of escape, they knocked Jenny Saint out and threw her off the top of a three-storey building." Her voice was sharp with controlled rage.

"The devil," Mrs. Baron Shaw said. "How bad is it?"

"Stephen managed to cushion her fall a bit, so she's not actually dead, but that's about as much as I can say. She has a fractured skull, her collarbone shattered like dropped china, she's broken her arm in two places. We don't know yet if her brain is damaged. She's in Bart's, with Dan trying to put her back together under the watchful eye of her fiancé, who, if I may remind you, works for—"

"Oh God, no," said Mrs. Baron Shaw.

"Quite. His lordship is apparently making his feelings known."

"If that man comes here…" Mrs. Baron Shaw paused, considering her options, and settled for, "Tell him I'm out. I assume Pastern and his accomplice are being sought?"

"There's not a justiciar in London doing anything else. Except me, obviously. If anyone wanted to commit a crime, this would be a wonderful time." Mrs. Gold glanced round at what was, by now, a reasonably large crowd of fascinated onlookers and added with lethal clarity, "I'd be grateful for an excuse."

That was enough to send Crispin, like quite a lot of the others, scurrying back to his abandoned work. So the unhappy prisoner, Spenser, had got away. He'd heard about that business: Spenser was the accomplice of the rogue windwalker Jonah Pastern, and in more than magical crime. Janossi had used various words to convey that; Crispin preferred *lovers*.

He had the picture, the drawing that tangled Spenser in intangible threads. Crispin pulled it out and traced the pencil lines with a finger.

He could draw over them, he was sure. He could bring those sagging cobweb lines of force alive, catch Spenser in their net once more, and Pastern with him. Pastern was a wanted man, accessory to murder. Crispin could win favour with the justiciary and prove himself to London practitioners. If he helped catch Pastern, he'd be a hero.

And Spenser, now fleeing the avenging justiciary, would find himself back in gaol. But they were bound to be caught anyway. The only difference would be Crispin getting a share of the glory.

He looked at Spenser's serious pencilled face a while longer. Then he sighed, shoved the paper under a pile of waste where nobody would find it, and settled back to his work.

He left the Council around six, tired and hungry but satisfied. His work had gone well. He wished he could go and tell Ned about it.

No, he didn't. He wished he could walk into the paper store and grab Ned's face in both hands, kiss him till he was laughing and breathless, and just *tell* him—

But he couldn't, because Ned was angry and right to be. Because he deserved better than empty words and meaningless promises. Because Crispin was going to Oxford.

He wanted Ned's respect. Other things too—laughing eyes and strong dusty fingers, the curve of his lips and the muscles of his absurdly powerful forearms—but he *needed* Ned's respect and he was aware in a sordid, truthful corner of his heart that he hadn't earned it. Hadn't, and wouldn't until he took charge of himself, instead of leaning on Ned's strength. But to do *that* he had to get his powers sorted out.

The fact was, he could stay here, fearful and unhappy and clinging, or go away and learn, and come back stronger and wiser. He might lose Ned either way, but at least one of those ways would leave him some dignity. You never knew, maybe Ned wouldn't have found someone new in a few years, maybe he'd still be there and Crispin could walk in with confidence…

Maybe he should stop expecting Ned to be the salve for his unhappiness.

He was hungry after the day's work. He stopped at a stall down the street for a few pieces of fried fish that came so hot the steam puffed from his mouth as he ate, wolfed down a full two pennies' worth of eel, relishing its glorious belly-filling richness rather more than the taste, and bought a "potato all hot" to fill up the crevices.

"Pleasure to serve a gent with an appetite," the stallkeeper said. "You won't stay that thin for long."

"You'd be amazed," Crispin said through a mouthful of potato. "Are those beef puddings you have there?"

"Ah, you might say beef, sir. You might well say that."

You didn't spend months with Ned without picking up a few things. Crispin gave the man a look. "I dare say I might. What would *you* say?"

The man snorted. "Mutton, then, but finely spiced. It's all one, ain't it? Once you get a good mix with the onion and a grind of pepper to take your head off, it's all one."

"And all things are from the One," Crispin agreed, and grinned at the blank look that got. He accepted the mutton pudding, paid up, and set off on the walk home again.

He was not at all sure he understood the lines Dr. Sweet had quoted, or agreed with what they seemed to say. The world never seemed one to him. It was a mess of contradictions and differences and jagged edges, lives unspooling in different directions, clashing and tangling and tying one another in knots. He didn't even feel one in his own head, not with fears and desires and obligations pulling him all ways at once. He couldn't do something as simple as hate Waterford or love Ned without it getting *complicated.*

He wondered if Ned ever felt like this. Maybe everyone did and they were all better at hiding it than Crispin.

He'd learned the words, though he had no idea what they meant, and he recited them mentally now, trying to understand. *And as all things are from the One, by the meditation of One, so all things have their birth from this One Thing by adaptation. The Sun is its Father, the Moon its Mother, the Wind carries it in its belly, its nurse is the Earth...*

No, it still sounded like a lot of nonsense. And anyway, if you wanted to talk about the four elements, who had decided that the moon represented water? You saw that in lots of old texts, witchcraft and alchemy, and it annoyed Crispin every time. For one thing, everyone knew the moon was made of earth, or at least rock; for another, the moon was all very well, but if you wanted a big, impressive thing to represent water, what was wrong with the sea? It seemed disrespectful to Crispin, Cornish to the bone, and you were disrespectful to the sea at your peril.

In fact, he reflected, if you wanted to talk of earth, air, fire, and water, the sea should be at the centre of it. Standing on a Cornwall clifftop, on earth shaped by the waves, with the sea wind in his hair, the great expanse of shifting grey-blue spread out before him and the setting sun blazing a path over the waves...*that* was as close to any mystical "One" as he'd ever come. That was earth, air, fire—

The last greasy corner of mutton pudding slipped from his hand.

Fire blazing through Voake. Earth filling the mouth of the other man. A woman suffocated, dead by air.

"*Shit,*" Crispin said aloud.

He had no idea how it fitted together, or how the jugs came into it, or what it meant. It didn't matter at this moment. What mattered was that there would have to be a death by water too, and it might not have happened yet because surely Ned would have heard about it, surely nobody could take a person drowned on their own floor as natural or accidental. Could they be in time to stop a death by water?

But the earth and fire deaths had happened almost two weeks ago, the suffocation last week. Why wait?

Crispin looked up at the sky. The moon, the full, bright, bloody bitch water moon, shone back at him.

"Oh no," he said on a breath, and started running.

He should have run in the direction of the Council. That would be the sensible thing. He should be running to Esther Gold, or Mrs. Baron Shaw; to Dr. Sweet, if he could find him. To *someone* who might be able to stop whatever the devil would happen when the jugs had claimed lives by earth, air, fire, and water.

Instead, and for no sensible reason at all, he was running as hard as he could towards Grape Street, running so his feet hurt with the impact on the pavement and his lungs hurt with the chill air, sliding on mud and jumping heaps of cabbage-stalks and straw, with nothing on his mind but getting to the rag and bottle, and Ned. He slipped and dodged and hurdled a fallen cart, swung round the corner to Grape Street without regard for the dank shadows that closed around him, scattered a ragged child's game of twigs, and skidded to an ungainly, gasping halt.

The door of the rag and bottle stood ajar. It should have been locked.

"I will kill you," Crispin said aloud, he wasn't sure to whom. "If you've come here, I will *kill* you." He shoved the door open. "Ned? Ned!"

Nothing. It felt empty inside, cold, dead. He ignited witchlight, careless of how it might look on the street, and his stomach plunged.

There were bottles and cans strewn on the floor, a gimcrack table half-overturned. A rickety shelf hung drunkenly from one support, its contents left where they had spilled. The door to the paper store stood open, and through it he could see the light of an oil lamp flicker.

Ned never left flames unattended in the paper store. Never.

"Ned!" Crispin shouted, and heard his voice echo flatly into the silence. "Ned!"

But there was nobody here. And when he looked up to the high shelf, he saw the Bellarmine jug was gone.

CHAPTER EIGHT

One more time. He was going to try this *one more time*, and it was going to work because there was no reason it shouldn't.

Ned took a deep breath, opened his mouth, and tried to shout.

It didn't come. He could feel the air stick in his throat, like a door slammed shut, but he couldn't force a bit of it out, no matter how hard he tried, and while he tried, he couldn't even breathe. It was the awful silencing of a nightmare, only he was awake, and he wished to hell this was a dream.

He tried again to force out the cry for help, but there were black spots gathering at the edge of his vision. He gasped air, hunkering down to a squatting position and ducking his head between his knees till he could see clear again.

He was in a deserted house of some kind. Or, at least, this room was empty, bare-walled, the floor dusty, with sticks of broken furniture, rusty nails and bits of brick scattered around. No table or chair; an empty grate. There was an old oil lamp, full, which he'd got burning, but that was it for signs of habitation. The windows were shuttered and the door shut, maybe bolted, but that didn't matter because, along with not being able to shout, Ned couldn't walk up to it. He could walk round the centre of the room, but it felt like there was an invisible wall set up a foot inside the actual walls, letting him go that far and not a step further. A wall that kept out sound too, because he couldn't hear the slightest noise from outside.

He'd been brought here, trapped and silenced by magic. That was undeniable, no matter how much he'd have liked to believe otherwise. Someone wanted him out of the way. Someone—and Ned did not feel at all chipper about this—was keeping him here on purpose.

Someone. The sod.

Ned had been in the paper store, stacking his latest load, when he heard noise from the rag and bottle. That was meant to be closed up, and just because Voake was dead didn't mean anyone could rob him, with Ned on the premises. So he'd headed through the connecting door, pushing his sleeves up in a meaningful sort of way, and seen a man standing there caressing that damn beardy jug like he loved it. *What the hell are you doing?* Ned remembered demanding, and the man had said, *Ned Hall?*

It was all a bit unclear after that. He'd tried to fight and was pretty sure he'd got a punch in, because his knuckles stung, but otherwise… He remembered the fellow's eyes, and then a sort of happy feeling, like everything was all right and there was no need to worry. A drifty, unreal sensation of movement, like walking in a dream, and a tiny part of his brain screaming at his body to wake up, wake up, *stop letting this happen!*

He hadn't.

He'd blinked awake after who knew how long to find himself in this room, with no idea where he was or how much time had passed, no means of calling for help, and no way out. And what was worrying him was, firstly, the fellow who'd caught him knew his name, as if he'd been looking for Ned particular, and secondly, he had to assume he was trapped here for a reason, and he was inclined to think he wouldn't like the reason when he heard it.

Face it. The weird deaths, the Bellarmine jugs, and the magician collecting them were all connected, and that same magician had collected Ned too, or he was a Dutchman. Ned had been after him, so he'd come after Ned first, and got him. And the chances of that ending well looked pretty slim.

Oh my days, Ned thought because he couldn't say it, and had a minute crouched there on the dusty floor, hiding his face from the empty room, because he was afraid.

One minute, and then he took another deep breath, shoved himself to his feet, and made himself look sharp.

A bit of hard thinking convinced him there wasn't anything of use in here. He couldn't get at the windows or the door. He had on him two lucifer matches, a grubby handkerchief, a wrap of twine, his flask with a mouthful of gin left in it, which was a pity because he'd rather have had water, a few sheets of paper folded together, a stub of pencil, and Crispin's pen.

Crispin.

Ned's gut twisted at the thought of how they'd parted. Would Crispin come back and find the paper store empty? Would he understand Ned hadn't vanished on purpose? Was he even all right himself? If Ned's investigations had brought trouble to Crispin's door and he'd left him defenceless without his pen…

Or maybe he'd never find out. Maybe Ned was going to be burned or choked on earth like those other poor sods and Crispin would never know what happened to him.

He wished he hadn't been such a prick yesterday. He should know better than to drink. He should know better than to make a fuss, come to that. Crispin had his magic, and Ned was only a waste-man, and he should have lived with how it was, instead of letting himself get tied up in knots about it. All he'd done was to spoil what had probably been their last meeting, the way things looked. He could have had that bit more time with Crispin, and he'd thrown it away like he didn't want it, instead of seeing what it was worth.

He wished he'd said goodbye properly. He didn't want whatever was going to happen to him anyway, but he *really* didn't want everything between him and Crispin to end like this, in lonely rooms and anger and loss.

If only he'd been able to see him once more, just to say…

He could leave a message. The thought came hard and bright. He'd write something down and maybe, possibly, if someone—justiciary?—came looking for him, they might see it. Maybe he could write something they could use, even; it would be something if they could get the sod who was behind all this. He'd have to be careful with what he said, not write anything the peelers could use against Crispin. But please God maybe he might see it, and if not, at least Ned would know he'd tried.

He unfolded the sheaf of paper, spread a sheet on the dusty floorboards, took the pencil stub, wrote *For Crispin Tred* at the top, and felt the lead snap.

He stared at the splintered wood. Well, that was it. The pencil was broken and he didn't have a pocketknife. He couldn't write Crispin a message, and the desperate loss clouded his eyes for a second. All he'd wanted was to say goodbye, and he didn't have a sodding thing to write with.

Except.

Except…

It probably wouldn't work. The damn thing wrote in Crispin's blood, which it tapped in some blasted magic way. It probably wouldn't do that for Ned, and there was nothing else to use for ink.

And if it *did* work… He remembered again that devil-pen that had worn the body of Crispin's master. A greedy man had claimed it and written with it, and the pen had swallowed his soul, just like that, and taken him with it when it was destroyed. Crispin's pen had no life of its own, as far as he knew, but what might happen if Ned wrote with it?

Would it be worse than whatever he was stuck in this silent cage waiting for?

Ned took the cap off the pen. The bone nib, made of Crispin's own finger, looked yellow-white. Writing with blood had never stained it.

He weighed the pen experimentally in his hand. The silver barrel was slightly warm—must be because it had been in his pocket, no other reason—and its carved decorations felt odd and a little uncomfortable in his grip.

It probably wouldn't work. He wasn't magic. In his hands it was nothing but a pen with no ink.

Oh well. Here goes.

He put the pen to the paper to finish writing Crispin's name, gave a silent yelp of pain, and snatched his hand away so hard the damn thing went flying from his fingers and rolled across the floor.

It had hurt like hell, like someone had jammed a toasting fork into his spine. He put his fingers to the back of his neck, expecting to feel the warm wet of blood, but there was only unbroken skin. He checked his fingers, saw nothing.

What there *was,* was a red *a* on the paper. He'd written in his own blood with Crispin's pen.

Ned contemplated that for a second, as the pain in his spine faded, then lunged to retrieve the pen from the floor with a dizzying burst of hope.

He'd seen Crispin unlock a door by writing; he knew it was possible. But Crispin wrote in Latin and drew little squiggle things around the words. Did you have to do those? Did magic only work in Latin? Did the words even matter? Crispin had said something about that, but it hadn't made a lot of sense then and Ned couldn't remember it now.

It was worth a try, though. He wrote *Open door,* wincing at the pain, and then *Magic go away,* because he had no idea how else to put it. He wasn't sure what he was expecting to happen, and it didn't feel as though he was doing anything except writing while being stabbed in the neck.

Well, here goes not a lot, he thought, and rose to see if anything had happened. He took a few steps forward, hand out, telling himself not to expect it, of course he couldn't do magic—

His hand hit solid nothing. The invisible walls were still there.

The brief surge of hope ebbed, leaving him with the bitter taste of irony. Crispin could have written them out of here with no trouble, but he wasn't here because Ned had sent him packing. And Ned had Crispin's pen, a magical weapon of absurd power, and all he could do with it was write a note.

Ned breathed hard for a moment then gave himself a nudge. Two minutes ago he'd been in despair because he didn't have anything to write with; now he did, so at least he could do that.

Right, start again. *To Crispin Tredarloe,* he wrote doggedly against the cold sensation of something draining from the top of his spine. This was the worst pen in the world. Crispin had to be balmy.

C—Give this to 'Freckles' for me, will you.

That was the best way he could think to write frankly without incriminating his lover. He'd understand.

Freckles—I got taken by one of your lot. Came for the jar, knew my name. Looked

The pen jerked to a halt. Ned glared at his hand, stuck still as the nib dug fruitlessly into the paper. He'd wanted to write a description of the bugger who'd taken him from the shop, but apparently he was silenced that way too because he couldn't move his damn fingers. Helpless fury swelled his chest. If he had a chance to get his hands on the sod who'd done this…

He should get the important stuff down while he had the chance. He took a deep breath and started again.

Trapped in room. Cant get out. Not so good. Sorry I shouted. I love you.

He looked down at the words he'd written, glistening red.

Your the best, Freckles. Wish Id told you. Hope you see this. I

His hand stopped again, jolting violently on the page. The pain in his neck spiked, sudden and fierce, and Ned felt a surge of panic because the pen was jerking in his hand, pulling it, *controlling*. Was this the possession starting?

Sod it. If this bloody pen was stealing his soul, it could have the good manners to wait till he'd finished his letter. Ned set his teeth, put the nib to the paper again, and felt it skid, dragging his hand sideways with startling force into a continuous scrawl of loops and spikes.

Why would the pen want to write gibberish like that? Did it have magic meaning? It looked almost like writing, in fact, except there was no such word as *nedareyouthere—*

Ned felt his mouth drop open as his mind resolved the scribble into meaning. His hand felt free now, able to move. He swallowed hard, and wrote, *Yes.*

There was a tiny pause, then the pen was dragging his hand across the paper again.

looseyourhand

Ned did his best to relax, which wasn't precisely easy. The pen was vibrating almost imperceptibly under his fingers, and there was an infuriating not-quite-there noise in his ears, as though the blasted thing was humming. The back of his neck hurt in a sick-making, dull, draining sort of way that felt profoundly wrong. He hated this, but he breathed out hard and let the pen drag his hand over the paper, and once it could move freely, the writing it produced was astonishingly, impossibly familiar.

It's Crispin. Are you all right?

Crispin. Crispin was writing to him, *with* him. He wasn't alone any more. Ned felt his body shudder in what was close to a silent sob, got a grip on himself.

Am fine but trapped

Where are you? How trapped?

Dont know where. In room. Cant shout. Cant reach walls.

?

Like I got to stop a foot away

Binding, Crispin wrote unhelpfully. *Who took you?*

Dont know. Ned fought the constriction again, gave up. *Cant write what* He couldn't even write "he", damn it. *Cant say anything.* A brainwave struck. *My knuckles hurt*

From the pen?

Ned raised his eyes to the ceiling. *No*

Pause. *You mean you hit him?*

He couldn't write *Yes*, hand hovering infuriatingly over the paper, but evidently Crispin took the silence as response. *Right. Can you see any way out?*

No. Can you find me?

Don't know. Wait

Ned watched the paper, keeping the pen loose. Nothing happened for long enough that he had to struggle to stop himself writing *Are you still there?* Crispin was doing something, or trying to.

He was there, on the other end of whatever connection this was, when Ned had feared he'd never see or speak to him again.

I love you Freckles. Should of said. I love you.

The pen leapt in his hand. *Me too so much.* It hesitated, came back to underline the last two words emphatically, darted off again. *Have you got your flask?*

What? *Yes*

We're going to make a witch bottle. Empty flask. Put in iron nails, dust, ash. Fine earth if you can. And long thin things, metal and organic

?

Alive/dead things. Bone, wood

Splinters?

Crispin ticked that. Ned tipped out the gin and scrabbled on the floor for what it seemed was needed. Rusty nails, shards of old wood, a scraping of brick dust and the contents of his pockets.

Done

Now fill w piss not quite full leave a space

Easy for you to say, Ned thought. He was painfully thirsty, and the mouth of the flask wasn't large, but he unbuttoned himself, got over to the far corner in case of spillage, and did his best.

Done

Got a fire?

No

The pen was wrenched before he could write more. *I might be able to light one, is there anything to burn we need f*

Ned clamped his fingers around the skidding pen, forcing his own words through. *Got 2 matches!*

Could have said. Light fire, put bottle on when burning. This will bring witch to you, in pain. Be ready.

Ned contemplated that prospect sourly for a moment, but they obviously didn't have any better ideas between them, so he hauled himself up to see about a fire. No shortage of old dry wood here. The problem was, he couldn't get to the grate: the invisible barrier, or binding, held fast. Ned considered that, then stood back and tossed a piece of wood experimentally. It turned out that as long as he let go of the wood quick enough, it would go through.

He threw the best kindling he could find into the grate, then dunked the end of his handkerchief in the oil of the lamp, tied it to a bit of kindling, struck one of his precious lucifers on the rough floorboard, and let it flame under the cloth. Then he tossed the stick through the invisible barrier to the grate—

And reached too bloody far, because his hand hit the barrier and stopped dead, and the stick dropped to the floor on the other side, smouldering uselessly on the floorboards.

Hell's bloody legions.

Ned stuck the end of a thin bit of wood in the oil, soaking it. He had one more match. He could throw the lamp if that failed, but then he'd be left in the dark, waiting for an angry witch.

Better not miss, then.

He lit his taper, lobbed the burning stick gently through and, *yes*, this time it hit the pile in the grate dead-on and stayed there. Within a few seconds, a piece of kindling spluttered to life. He stood, watching as though the flames depended on his supervision, and saw them catch and leap. A few more bits of kindling, a couple of larger bits of wood, another minute, and he had a blaze. A blaze in the grate and, he couldn't help but note, a stick that was still burning in front of it, on the floor.

Worry about that later. Now for the thing he couldn't get wrong. If he missed this, he was buggered. Ned picked up the flask, unpleasantly warm to his touch and a little damp, took a couple of careful practice swings, and threw it onto the fire.

Bull's-eye.

Bit of a shame the stick aflame on the floorboards looked like it wasn't going out. More of a shame he'd nothing to put it out with and no way to reach it. Well. He'd better hope whatever was going to happen would happen faster than the fire spread.

He gave the flask an admonitory glare, in case it dared fall out of the grate, then hurried back to the paper. He'd sort of thought it might have acquired more writing in his absence, another message, but of course it couldn't, with no hand holding the pen.

He grabbed the silver barrel and felt the daggerlike stab in his neck once more. It was beginning to make him feel a bit dizzy and very hungry. No wonder Crispin was such a wraith.

Bottle on fire, he wrote. *Now what?*

There was quite a long pause. Ned stayed there, crouched on the floor, waiting, for lack of anything else to do, looking between the paper and the fire.

At last his hand moved.

The pen wrote, *He's coming*

CHAPTER NINE

Put bottle on when burning.

Crispin held his pencil poised for a moment in case Ned needed further instructions, then sat back, hand shaking, to wait.

It was past nine o'clock, and the Council was virtually empty. The justiciars were all still absent, combing London for the fugitives Pastern and Spenser. Crispin had come here after leaving the rag and bottle in the hope of finding Mrs. Gold, since she at least might listen to his tale, or Dr. Sweet, who he was sure would help, but neither was to be found. That had left him with no ideas at all except to return to Dr. Sweet's study and see if he could discover anything about elemental deaths. It felt like old practice, like witchcraft, and as such Dr. Sweet would surely have some useful book to consult.

He hadn't found anything like that. There was, however, a copy of a recent scholarly pamphlet by Dr. Sweet himself on the principles of witch bottles. Crispin had grabbed that, since he didn't have any better ideas. It had actually been quite interesting, explaining the resonant and representational magics that lay behind the practice in surprisingly clear language for a theoretical text, and he'd been halfway through reading it when his pen hand had begun to twitch. *Really* twitch, his thumb and first fingers closing into a familiar shape, his hand jerking, wrist flexing. As though he were writing.

He had never experienced any such thing before, and he felt an instinctive surge of panic at the alien sensation controlling his hand. The compulsion to find out what was going on was stronger. He grabbed a pencil from the desk, put it to the nearest sheet of paper, and then sat staring at his own hand as it traced ungainly, rounded, familiar letters.

Trapped in room. Cant get out. Not so good.

"Ned?" he said aloud.

Sorry I shouted.

"Ned!"

I love you.

Crispin's heart gave a single thump that shook the blood in his ears. Then he was whispering "yes, oh God, me too, me too" in an urgent undertone and wondering what the devil he could do—

Wish I'd told you. Hope

He could write, that was what. Crispin tightened his grip on the pencil, pouring in the power and bending all his will on the connection, not even daring to lift the point off the paper to separate the words as he wrote *nedareyouthere*, and prayed with all his heart that his writing would be read.

And now Ned was making a witch bottle.

Crispin had had to pause to consult the pamphlet, rather than relying on his memory or Janossi's expertise, but it seemed a fairly simple procedure. Iron for blood, dust and shards for flesh and bone, earth, water, and air all going on the fire, and the ensorcelled victim's body waste to bind the charm.

Ned wasn't a practitioner, but he almost certainly didn't need to be for old craft. That was one of the reasons it had been so firmly stamped out: practitioners preferred to keep power to themselves. That, and because the results of using witch bottles were not pretty.

Crispin pushed a flop of hair back from his eyes. His hand felt shaky.

If this worked, as the witch bottle heated, the sorcery would turn back on its caster. It wouldn't break the binding that trapped Ned, but it would, or should, bring the practitioner who'd bound him in agony to the door. Ned was a strong man, he'd have the advantage of knowing what was going on, and if he was ready with a stick, he could surely knock his captor over the head.

If he didn't take the bottle off the fire before it exploded, the witch would die.

Crispin didn't want to kill anyone. Even a murderer, even someone with unholy designs on Ned. Crispin did not want blood on his hands. But if he told Ned the witch bottle could kill, there was a better-than-even chance he would take it off the fire in case, and if he did that, he'd be facing an angry practitioner whom he'd just caused a great deal of pain.

Crispin gazed irresolutely at the paper. Ought he tell Ned, give him the choice? Or should he take the responsibility himself, and make Ned an accessory to—

To a death. It *wouldn't* be murder, not under the circumstances. It would serve the practitioner right, Crispin told himself, and wondered how the justiciary did it. Stephen Day hadn't looked uncertain, storming through the Council halls, gripping a warlock's severed head by the hair. How did anyone feel that sure of their actions?

But in the end, he didn't have to feel sure, or right, or even good. He simply had to do whatever would keep Ned safe. And if that meant not telling him that what he was doing might kill… Well, Crispin would face the consequences later.

Worried, twitchy, sick at heart, he was waiting with the pencil poised and wishing Ned would write something, when he heard footsteps in the corridor outside. It was half past nine. Why was anyone except him here?

He tensed, holding himself ready, and called, "Hello?"

"Crispin?"

Crispin sagged back in relief. "Dr. Sweet!"

"Good heavens, you're here late." Dr. Sweet came in, turning away to hang up his topcoat. "What are you doing?"

"I'm so glad you're here," Crispin said in a rush. "I need your help, Doctor."

Dr. Sweet turned back, an expression of concerned curiosity on his kindly face, and Crispin's stomach lurched as though he'd eaten a bad oyster. *No,* he thought, as the chair seemed to sway under him. *No, no, no.*

"Crispin? What is it?"

"I, uh, found out how to use my powers a new way." His mouth felt like it belonged to someone else. "I thought you could help me get it right. What happened to your face?"

Dr. Sweet put a hand to the dark-red mark under his eye, too recent to be a bruise yet. "Oh, a mere accident." He chuckled ruefully. "I was careless. It's nothing at all, dear boy. Now, it is rather late, and I do have some work to complete tonight, but if you'd like to tell me what you've discovered…?"

"No, no it's nothing," Crispin said mechanically. "It'll wait. I won't keep you from your work." His pen hand twitched violently. He pressed it hard against the desk.

"Well, I must admit it would be ideal if I could tackle this tomorrow," Dr. Sweet said with a smile. "I'd love to help, but I can't delay my own work. Still, tomorrow, I can—" His brows drew together, a sharp movement. "I can very happily—" He gave a sudden sucking gasp.

Ned's flask was cheap, thin tin. On a fire, it would heat up very quickly. "Dr. Sweet? Does something hurt?"

"Heartburn, I think." Dr. Sweet was going unpleasantly pale. "Don't mind…me. I—ah!"

"You don't look well," Crispin said, with a calm he couldn't quite feel was his own. "You probably need to deal with the pain, don't you?"

Dr. Sweet's lips drew back, revealing large yellow-white teeth in a snarl that distorted his scholarly features. He angled his neck unpleasantly, shoulder rising and twisting, then jerked forward as though he'd been kicked in the back. Crispin recoiled in his chair. Dr. Sweet gave him a single frantic glare from white-rimmed eyes, turned with a gargling noise, and fled the room.

He'd be going to wherever Ned was trapped.

Crispin scrawled *He's coming* on the paper. He snatched up the pencil, a couple of sheets of paper, and the witch-bottle pamphlet, and ran like hell, pulling on his coat as he went.

He rattled down the stairs of the Council two at a time, swung through the hallway, and almost collided with Mrs. Gold.

"Sorry!" he yelped, trying to dodge round her immense belly, and found his arm seized.

"Tredarloe? What's going on?"

"I've got to go!" He wrenched fruitlessly at her grip.

She tightened her grip. "I just saw Dr. Sweet looking like death on foot. *What* is going on?"

Crispin hesitated for a second, cycling through options with frantic haste. "I need a justiciar, an active one."

"Everyone's looking for the swine who attacked Saint."

"Other people matter too," Crispin said through his teeth. "People have been killed, someone else may be murdered tonight. I need help! Janossi, Mr. Day—"

"Both on their way to Reading. Talk to me. Let me see what I can do."

It was notorious that her pregnancy meant she couldn't do anything, and Crispin had no time to waste. "I think Dr. Sweet is a murderer. I'm going to stop him. Let me *go*." He pulled again, as hard as he dared, and this time Mrs. Gold released him.

He shot out of the big doors into Lincoln's Inn Fields, frantically looking around, and made out a dark silhouette moving in a jerky, wounded way over on the other side of the square. Crispin sprinted after him, praying he was right, and caught up with the tall, hatless, coatless figure as Dr. Sweet stumble-ran past the Courts of Justice. Crispin slackened his pace a little, keeping behind, following down Chancery Lane to the Strand and Fleet Street, both brightly gaslit and still busy with hurrying workers, late revellers, stalls, and hawkers. Dr. Sweet ran with a spasmodic sideways motion, flailing his arms in a way that had passersby objecting loudly.

Dr. Sweet. Dr. bloody Sweet. It was just as Ned said: you couldn't trust practitioners. They were all stupid, horrible, selfish, monstrous people, and whatever was happening to Dr. Sweet was no more than he deserved.

Dr. Sweet let out an awful sobbing shriek of pain. Crispin told himself fiercely that the tears in his eyes were the cold, and ran onward.

Down New Bridge Street, and past Ludgate Hill station, bright with gas lamps, dark with men in suits and coats. Crispin briefly lost Dr. Sweet in the crowd, even at this time of night, but all he had to do was listen for that whooping scream. He caught up at the turning to Queen Victoria Street, running under the dank, cold arches of the railway viaduct, taking the left fork down Upper Thames Street.

They were going to Puddle Dock. To the river. It was a full moon, and the Thames was at the full too, the high tide rushing in. He could smell the sea from here. If you wanted a death by water, how better to do it than under a full moon and a high tide?

If Dr. Sweet had meant Ned for that death, Crispin would…well, he wouldn't be sorry about the witch bottle. Not at *all*.

He was almost on the man's heels now. He could hear the harsh gargling breaths, see the way Dr. Sweet's shoulders plunged as his legs nearly gave way. He was moving more like a dead man walking than a live one, and Crispin wished he wasn't able to make that comparison.

Dr. Sweet lurched to the right into the dark, forbidding, tar-rot-river stink of Crown & Horseshoe Wharf. There was no gas lighting here, and the stunted buildings leaned at disturbing aggressive angles, jutting overhead, blocking the moonlight. Dr. Sweet made a headlong lunge at a door and scrabbled at it, breath coming in short, horrible gasps.

It didn't look like he could open it. He wasn't even trying, in fact, just scratching feebly at the wood. Crispin came up behind him, wary, but Dr. Sweet didn't seem to notice him. He didn't seem in a state to notice anything.

Crispin had just started wondering what he should do now when the other smell crept into his awareness.

Smoke. The building smelled of smoke.

Crispin shoved his way forward, pushing the doctor aside, and rattled the door handle. It was locked. "Keys!" he shouted, and saw no glimmer of understanding in Dr. Sweet's glaring, tortured eyes. He jammed his hands in the man's pockets, searching frantically, but of course Dr. Sweet had left his coat back at the Council. If he only had his pen—

He could do this. He *knew* he could.

Crispin shut his eyes, pulling calm from somewhere. He fished the pencil from his pocket, shoved the sobbing Dr. Sweet aside, and touched it to the door.

I write the world as I want it to be. I write, and it is.

Recludam, he pencilled on the wood, and the door swung open, letting out a soft billow of smoke.

Crispin had a second of disbelieving joy, then another of confusion as Dr. Sweet pushed him out of the way, sending him stumbling over next door's bootscraper. He picked himself up and bolted inside, witchlight blooming around him, in time to see Dr. Sweet wrench open a door. He stumbled in, and there was an almighty, solid, concussive crack, followed by a thump.

"Ned!" Crispin shrieked, taking two long strides to the doorway. Dr. Sweet was facedown on the floor, not moving. The room behind was bright with flame and dark with smoke.

"*Freckles?*" Ned appeared from his ambush position behind the door, dropping the piece of wood he held, and pulling down the neckerchief tied over his mouth and nose. "Freckles!"

Crispin leapt over Dr. Sweet's body and collided with Ned, hugging harder than he'd have thought himself able. Ned, solid alive Ned, reeking of smoke, holding him right back and kissing his ear and hair frantically. "Oh God, Ned, you're all right. Are you all right? Tell me you're all right."

"Fine. I think." Ned pushed his face into Crispin's shoulder, gripping so tight it actually properly hurt, and Crispin didn't care. Ned, safe and holding on to *him*. "Oh my days. You're here. You came."

"I— Oh my God." Crispin jerked back. "The witch bottle!"

"Burning," Ned assured him. "So's everything else. We got to go."

Crispin took in the situation in the room for the first time. The fire in the grate was blazing, and so was the floor in front of it, floorboards well aflame. He could just make out the glowing metal of Ned's flask, white-hot on the fire.

"Hell's teeth!" He dropped to his knees—the wood under him was too warm—grabbed his pencil and wrote *Extinctio* on the plank.

It was like punching a brick wall. He dropped the pencil, shaking his hand, as the universe declined to be rewritten. He wasn't strong enough, not like this…

"Pen!" he yelped, coughing on the acrid smoke. Ned shoved it into his hand without question, and Crispin didn't even have to look as he scrawled *Extinctio* again and felt the pen bite.

The fire went out so suddenly that its absence left afterimages flickering in his eyes.

"Bloody hell," Ned said hoarsely. "Did you—"

Dr. Sweet's body convulsed as an ominous creaking, ticking noise came from the grate. Crispin turned to see the little flask glowing too brightly to look at on a heap of embers, and realised that he'd put the flames out, but done nothing about the residual heat.

Frigidus, he scrawled so hard he felt the icy drain of the pen all the way down his back and in his hips, and then it was cold. The charred floor, the grate, the tin flask were dull and blackened, as if there had been a fire months ago.

Dr. Sweet made little gasping noises. Crispin wasn't sure if he was conscious.

"Swipe me," Ned said.

"Maybe later," Crispin said, and saw the laugh spark in Ned's eyes with a rush of joy and relief that brought tears to his own. "Oh God, Ned. Oh God."

Ned was down on the floor by him, holding him close, dropping kisses over his cheek and jaw. "You're a marvel, Freckles. A bloody marvel."

"I'm not. I'm so stupid." Crispin dashed at his wet eyes with the back of his hand. "I nearly made the worst mistake of my life. Again."

Ned pulled away to look at him, frowning. "What d'you mean?"

God, he didn't want to admit this. "Look, would you check if—he—is the man who kidnapped you?"

Ned glanced at Dr. Sweet's body, rose, and went over. Crispin kept his pen poised. If Dr. Sweet tried anything…

He seemed to be unconscious. Ned lifted his head cautiously by the hair, squinted at his face, let him go. "That's the fellow. Turned up in the rag and bottle, he'd got hold of the jug thing. Asked if I was Ned Hall, and then…made me come here." He grimaced at what was obviously a disturbing memory. "So he'll be the fellow behind this, right? He put me in here, and maybe he's the chap who bought the jug off Mrs. Reed too. Any idea who he is? Come to that, any idea how he knew my name?"

"Because I told him," Crispin said wretchedly. "He's Dr. Sweet."

"Doctor—your Dr. Sweet? Oh, you're joking. Oh, Freckles." The aching sympathy in his voice made Crispin's eyes fill. Dr. Sweet had been taking him away, and Ned still cared. He stood, walking into a fierce hug, and felt Ned's hand come up to cup the back of his skull, pulling him closer. "You have the worst luck."

"No, I don't," Crispin said into his shoulder. "For one thing, this isn't luck, it's a pattern. For another, I've got you. Or, at least—"

"You got me," Ned said. "When I thought I wasn't going to see you again…"

"I know. I *know*."

"There's a lot of things I should have said. Some I shouldn't." Ned's fingers were so tight, arms so strong round his waist. "Listen, Freckles, I know you've got things to do, your magic. I don't want to stop you—"

"I do," Crispin said. "I mean, I can't not be magic. I have to learn how to control it and use it and all that. But I am *sick* of this. I don't want to be part of it any more. I trusted him, and I told him your name and he went to kill you. It's not even the first time, is it? If being a practitioner means being an untrustworthy, selfish bastard—and I was going to go to Oxford and leave you behind—"

"Sssh." Ned rested his forehead against Crispin's. "'S all right. Or, no, it ain't, it's a country mile from all right. *You're* all right."

"I'm going to be." Crispin pulled himself straight. "So are you. But Mr. Voake, and Mr. Reed, and that poor dead woman—"

"Who?"

"The other rag'n'bottler, the one you found out about. I think we've had three murders, not two. And they weren't just murders. They were sacrifices."

"Sacrifices?" Ned looked appalled. He was an occasional churchgoer, not a particularly devout man, but Crispin knew that *ungodly* was more than just a word to him. "Sacrifices to what? For what?"

"I don't know. Maybe he was trying to make the jugs stronger, or maybe it was how he found out where they were, or both."

"But Voake burned almost a fortnight back, and Sweet only came for his jug today," Ned objected.

"After I'd told him where it was. I'm not sure he knew before then. He told me he was halfway to success, and that was after the air death. Maybe I disrupted the first sacrifice by putting the fire out? Or maybe he didn't mean to invoke earth and fire together, and Mr. Voake's death was an accident?"

Ned looked over at Dr. Sweet's recumbent form with an expression that boded no good to him. "An accident. Right."

"I'm guessing," Crispin said hastily. "It's a mess of old craft and goodness knows what and I've no idea how he was doing it. But we know for sure that there were earth and fire deaths when all this began; air a week later. I'm positive he planned a death by water too, and there's a full moon and a high tide tonight, which is exactly when you'd want to do that. I think he was going to…you know." He couldn't say it, not looking into Ned's eyes.

"He was going to sacrifice *me*? Drown me?"

"Yes." Crispin didn't care one bit that his voice cracked. "I told him everything you'd found out, and it looks like he decided he had to get rid of you. I'm so sorry."

Ned pulled him close again, as much taking comfort as giving it. "You weren't to know. You came after me."

"I just had to follow him. He was right there in the Council *talking* to me when the effects started." Crispin swallowed. "He told me he had work to do."

"Well." Ned's voice was a little shaky too. "Glad he didn't get round to it. Never liked the idea of drowning much, it's one reason I don't miss the docks." He took a deep breath. "Right, so what now? I clobbered him pretty hard, but he's still breathing. I got some twine, should we tie him up? Take him to the justiciary?"

"There's nobody around tonight. They're busy."

"The coppers are busy?" Ned repeated with some incredulity.

"There's an escaped murderer, a practitioner. They're out looking for him."

"Just how many— Never mind."

"The thing is," Crispin said, "if it comes to a fight with magic, Dr. Sweet's going to be better than me. And tying him up wouldn't be any use, unless we used iron, like chains or cuffs."

"Left mine at home." Ned was looking at Dr. Sweet with a frown creasing his brow. "Can you sort of trap him, like he did me?"

"I've no idea how."

"We got to do something with him. We know he killed those people from a distance, so if there needs to be a death by water to finish the job, who's to say he can't do it from here? Or what if he was working with someone else? We can't just leave him, and we can't wait around for your justiciary to pitch up, either. Someone's got to put a stop to this business."

"Yes." Crispin knew his voice sounded hollow. "Putting a stop to this" sounded alarming, possibly dangerous, definitely not something he knew how to do. The thought made his stomach squirm with a miserably familiar sense of apprehension.

But he knew what the man he wanted to be would do. And he'd damn well saved Ned's life, and Ned was looking at him as though he believed Crispin might have some answers, and maybe, actually, earning respect started here.

He set his shoulders. "Yes, you're right. Well, then, we'd better find the Bellarmine jugs. They're the key to this, aren't they?"

Ned nodded. "If he was going to, uh, sacrifice me, does that mean the things are here? In this house?"

"I suppose they could be." Crispin attempted to sound as though that might be a good thing. "Let's look."

"Should we split up, do it quicker?"

"No. Definitely not."

Ned grinned briefly. "Glad you said that." He glanced around, and swooped on a bit of paper with writing scrawled across it in dried blood. "Better not leave that lying about." He folded it, very carefully, and put it in his pocket. "Right, let's be getting on."

They left Dr. Sweet on the floor, still not moving. He'd bled quite a lot from a scalp wound where Ned had hit him. Another person might have suggested hitting him again, harder, and that might have been the most practical solution, but Crispin could not, and he was glad that Ned did not.

Instead, he shut the door on his unconscious mentor and spent a few minutes writing him asleep and the room closed as best he could before they set off to search the house.

CHAPTER TEN

Ned wasn't any more excited about looking round the house than Crispin obviously felt. He was thirsty as hell, his throat dry and scratchy from smoke and the effort of trying to shout and having his voice stopped. Bloody Dr. Sweet. But there was work to be done, so he got on and did it.

The house wasn't large, with one other room downstairs, empty, plus a tiny kitchen-scullery that held nothing of any use except a pump. Ned gulped water gratefully. Upstairs, one room held a couple of empty travelling boxes; the other a writing desk and a bookcase.

He turned in a circle, frustrated. There was nothing here but spiderwebs and damp. "This is no go. Maybe he was storing the jugs somewhere else, to bring here?"

"Maybe." Crispin frowned. "I didn't see them in the study at the Council—not that it would have been very clever of him to bring them there—and he didn't have a bag or anything with him when he came in. Perhaps he kept them at home? I could probably find out where he was lodging in London. But why would he have a hideaway like this and bring you here, and keep the jugs somewhere else?" He squatted to examine the bookcase, peering at the spines. "I mean, these are obviously his books, and… Good grief."

"What?" Ned came up to look over his shoulder.

"I can see why he didn't keep these in the Council building, that's all. He's got the *Kirtlington Receipts*."

"Is that bad?"

"It's not good. Rather nasty old practice, the witch-bottle sort of stuff. You're certainly not supposed to leave it lying around. What else… *A History of Oxfordshire Witchcraft 1727–1830. Practitioners of Oxfordshire. Early Georgian Witchcraft.* What's this?" He pulled out a book with a plain unmarked spine, flicked through the first few pages, and half-dropped, half-threw it onto the desk. "Jumping Judas!"

"What is it?" Ned reached for the book.

"Don't!" Crispin grabbed his wrist. "Just…best not. It's, uh, it's *Liber Revenienses*. Nobody is supposed to have that. Jumping *Judas*."

He sounded genuinely appalled and rather scared. Ned looked down at the plain tan leather. "What's wrong with it? What's it about?"

"Necromancy."

Ned sighed. "Throw a dog a bone, Freckles."

"Sorry. It's, uh, well, a kind of magic that… You know what happened to Mr. Foster?" He was the dead man that Mr. Marleigh had set walking through St. George's market last summer, a topic on which Ned had very strong feelings. "That sort of thing. But, um, worse."

Ned stared at the book. "How worse?"

"Well, warlockry." Crispin wiped his hands on his trousers which, given their state, wasn't going to be much help. "Using other people's blood and bone and life to call up the dead, animate corpses, that sort of thing. It's really not allowed. If you find a copy of this, you're meant to hand it in to the justiciary for burning, and honestly, practitioners don't usually burn books. It's *bad*. Wicked, I mean." He grimaced. "Some people say all the copies are bound in human skin."

It looked like normal leather to Ned, and there was nothing on the outside to suggest it was particularly evil. Still, there was no way he was picking it up, even to put it back on the shelf, still less opening it. "Urgh. So Sweet's a warlock, then?"

"Well, he's certainly got the library for it. What else... Trismegistus, unexpurgated. I *thought* that was bad. *Sympathetic Magic.*"

"That sounds all right," Ned said. "I could do with a bit of sympathy right now."

"Not that kind of sympathy. It means the connection between things that stand for things and the things." Ned gave him the look that deserved. Crispin waved his hands. "I mean—look, take the witch bottle. That works by sympathetic magic on the body of the witch. So the long, thin things represent bone, the dust is the body, the iron is blood, and it works by sympathy, or you could call it amplified etheric resonance."

"Shall we not?"

"You use a bottle and put it on the fire because witch bottles were originally used for storing the, uh, ashes after a witch was burned. It's all connected, you see." He illustrated that with a bit more hand-waving, up and down. "As above, so below."

None of that made much sense to Ned, and the bits he understood, he didn't like. "Storing the ashes of a burned witch in a bottle? Why would you do that?"

"Oh, to stop them coming back from the dead," Crispin said easily, and then his expression changed. They looked at each other for a moment of long, suspended silence.

"Right," Ned said at last. "Freckles. How old would you say those jugs were? Because I'd have said well over a century. And...Sweet's from Oxford, right?"

They both looked at *A History of Oxfordshire Witchcraft 1727–1830* where it sat on the shelf, and *Liber Revenienses* on the desk.

"Dr. Sweet's a specialist," Crispin said slowly. "He wrote a pamphlet, it's where I got all that stuff about the bottles. It said that sometimes, if it was a really bad witch, they'd split the ashes between several bottles." He sounded as hollow as Ned felt. "I suppose you'd need to strengthen the witch, warlock, whoever was in the bottle, if you wanted to bring them back."

"And you'd do that by sacrifices, would you?"

"Probably. Feeding it, you see. Making it strong."

"Yes. Right." Ned felt as though he was skirting the edge of a very deep pit. He glanced at the poisonous bookshelf again, and something caught his eye. "There's a bookmark there." He reached for *A History of Oxfordshire Witchcraft 1727–1830* and paused. "This human skin?"

"I shouldn't think so."

"Good." He hoicked the book out and onto the desk, opening it at the bookmark. The pages fell open there, as if the book was used to it.

The words were set in blurry black-letter type, the kind you could barely make out what the different letters were. That came through his paper store occasionally, old hymnals and the like. He wasn't a bad reader, given a bit of time, but he hadn't a hope of deciphering this. He could make out the inky woodcut, though: a man tied to a big stick, flames licking all round him. "Can you read it?"

Crispin nodded, peering at the incomprehensible type. "Let me see." His lips moved slightly, eyes flicking over the text, and Ned saw them widen. "Right. Um. It's about a man called John Kibble, a herbalist and a warlock of great power. It says here he could turn himself into a hare—"

"Really?"

"Well, it really says so. I don't suppose he could actually *do* it. Some practitioners are very good at controlling bodies outside themselves, though."

"Like when Sweet made me walk here?"

"That sort of thing. Perhaps that's what he did with the hare. Anyway, it didn't do him any good because it says he was trapped by a cunning man. That's the people who looked after things before the justiciary. And…oh Judas. It says he was burned, and they split the ashes between four witch bottles and 'thus his soul was torn and scattered to the four elements and the corners of the earth'. That's what it says."

"Well. Sounds like you're right about the elements, then. We need to get on and find those bottles, sharpish. Can you…?" He made a scribbling motion.

Crispin's jaw tightened. "I'll try."

Something was changing. Ned wasn't quite sure what it was, but he could feel it. He dickered over ha'pennies for a living and to do that you had to pay attention to people. Where they'd shift or give, where they hid. He could tell Crispin had crossed a line of some sort in his head, and Ned would have liked to know what it was.

Crispin wouldn't strike anyone as a tough sort. Some might call him pansyish, even, what with he wouldn't be the first into a fight, talked light, wore his feelings on his sleeve. Ned didn't see a problem with any of that. So what if Crispin cried easy? Ned's father had prided himself on being the toughest mother's son on the docks, and had probably never shed a tear in his life. He'd used gin and his fists to vent his feelings instead. If that was manly, Ned would rather have a molly.

And *also*, if you were going to draw comparisons, Crispin could probably melt Ned's old man into bubbling pond-water with a scratch of his pen, so who's harder now, Pa?

No, Ned liked his soft-voiced Freckles as he was, except that it drove him to Bedlam how down on himself he was. He'd sit there saying he wasn't good enough, and all Ned could think was, *Mate, you're the best thing I've ever had.* He'd hoped and prayed Dr. Sweet could change that, even while he'd been twisting up inside with…well, jealousy, let's be honest, and misery at what he knew was going to happen: Crispin, with his marshlight eyes, slipping out of his life like a will-o-the-wisp into a world of magic, a world that wasn't for the likes of Ned and where he couldn't follow.

And then he'd written *I love you* because he'd never managed to say it, even before he'd been silenced, and Crispin…

Me too so much. That was what he'd written. Ned had tried to pretend he'd snatched up that bit of paper for discretion, but it had been nothing of the sort, and he was fairly sure Crispin knew that. He'd just wanted those words to look at again.

Funny, really. A man could write a thing and even if he didn't have Crispin's powers, sometimes the world changed anyway.

He watched Crispin, sat scribbling at the desk, his dirty-blond hair glinting gilt in the light of an oil lamp he'd lit, and wondered if that was what had altered for them both.

The plain fact was that he didn't want Crispin to go to Oxford or anywhere, because he'd take everything that mattered with him, and leave Ned nothing but waste. And maybe it was selfish to say so, but it had been a flat-out lie to keep it silent. Crispin had needed to know, and Ned should have seen that.

He ought to say it in words. Ought to tell him the truth and talk it out between them and admit what he wanted. The thought was a little bit terrifying.

Anyway, he couldn't. Crispin was busy, and Ned did not plan to distract him. The idea of something, someone, whatever was in those bottles *coming back…* He did not want to find out what that meant. So he'd just have to leave saying anything for now. There'd be time enough later.

Crispin made a frustrated noise, pushing a piece of paper out of the way. He was writing with a pencil, Ned noticed. "Blast it. I can't work this out. I don't know what to do."

"Keep trying," Ned said. "I've seen you do any amount of impossible things, so why not this?"

"Because it's not *working*." Crispin slapped the pencil down and shoved both hands through his hair. "Goodness knows how much power those blasted jugs have. Anyone else would be able to sense them from a mile off and I can't!"

"Can you make them sing?" Ned suggested. "I mean, if they're here, I might hear them."

"I *tried*. It's like everything I do is shouting into an abyss. I can't find anything at all. Maybe we ought to go to the justiciary, demand somebody comes here. I bet one of them could help."

There was that miserable, self-loathing twist in his voice again. Ned dropped a hand to his shoulder and gave it a squeeze. "Come on, Freckles. You're the one who's managed everything so far. It's not like your man Janossi noticed anything odd about the jug when he had it in his hands and a body under his feet, did he? Nobody's perfect."

"But," Crispin began, and stopped. "Uh. Ned?"

"What?"

"You're right. Janossi was there, holding the jug, and he couldn't sense what killed Mr. Voake or my blood magic or anything else because there was nothing in the ether. And do you remember how the body, Mr. Voake's body, was so small?"

"Yeah?" Ned said cautiously, because the expression on Crispin's face was pretty odd.

"Well, I just wondered," Crispin said. "Suppose the jugs, the warlock—John Kibble's spirit, if that's what it is—suppose they were consuming things to get stronger. The traces of magic. Mr. Voake's body."

Ned thought about that. "What, like, so they sort of ate the magic you left behind? Poor old Voake too?"

"Soaked it all up and left nothing behind and that's why Janossi couldn't see it. That, uh, that's what I'm wondering. Yes."

He was on the verge of panic, Ned could see that, and he didn't feel any too steady himself as Crispin's meaning dawned on him. "So the reason you can't find them with magic might be because they're eating what you're doing?"

"And we could be right on top of them now."

"Uh-huh," Ned said. "Well. Good to know. So, what about the magic you locked Sweet in with?"

Crispin scrabbled in his pocket and pulled out a sheet of paper. His eyes widened as he turned it over and back. "It's gone. The writing's *gone*."

They bolted down the stairs, almost on top of each other. The door was still shut. Ned cast around in the hope of a handy bit of wood or suchlike to use as a club, saw nothing, and met Crispin's eye with a shrug. Crispin was clutching pencil and paper. He gave Ned a small nervous nod, and Ned put his hand to the doorknob and shoved the door open.

He was ready to jump, ready to move, ready to hit. He wasn't ready for what he saw. Nobody could have been, and it took a few seconds for his eyes to make sense of it.

"Crispin!" he screamed. "He's drowning!"

Dr. Sweet was thrashing on the floor, on his back, hands to his throat. His eyes were wide and blind with panic, and there was water gouting out of his mouth, out of his nostrils, as though it was pouring from inside him. He was trying to cough, the muscles of his throat spasming violently; his face was bloated with lips and eyelids a terrible livid colour, and his chest was swelling.

Ned hit the ground by him, rolling him over. He'd seen half-drowned men at the docks, he knew you had to get the water out, but it just kept coming, splashing in great bursts from Sweet's mouth as he jerked and retched. "Hell's bells. Crispin!"

"Do *not* try to give him air." Crispin sounded savage. "Don't get that water in your mouth."

Ned gripped on to Dr. Sweet, glaring up at Crispin because a man was drowning in his arms on a wood floor, and even as he thought that, Sweet gave a great convulsive spasm and stopped struggling.

"Oh bugger." Crispin clutched pencil and paper, white-faced. "Is he dead?"

"Shush a second." Ned could hear something faint, growing in volume as he listened. A familiar plaintive melody in a deep voice coming from under them. "Oh my days, it's 'Scarborough Fair'. From the cellar?"

Crispin scrawled something with his pencil and took off running, colliding with Ned as they both tried to get through the doorway at once. He was following his ears, which was absurd for a sound that wasn't there; heaven knew what Crispin was following, but they found themselves in the scullery together, looking down at the floor.

"Coal cellar," Ned said, realising. "The hole'll be at the front."

Crispin grabbed his arm. "Ned, this is bad, really bad. And you don't have any powers. Could you, uh, go?"

"What? No!" Ned could hear that bloody deep voice soaring, triumphant. *Then she'll be a true love of mine...* "We got to stop it."

"I do. You can't." Crispin looked sick as a dog. "I'm scared it'll hurt you."

"Piss off," Ned said flatly. "I'm not leaving you here, you berk. Come on."

They tumbled out of the front door into the dark, dank passage of Crown & Horseshoe Wharf, skidding on nameless stuff that slithered and stank underfoot. The water was right up round the planks of the quay as it jutted into the Thames, sparkling black in the moonlight, and Ned could hear the splash in his ears and the singing in his head.

Tell her to wash it in yonder dry well

Parsley, sage, rosemary and thyme...

"Shut up!" Ned snarled at it. "What's that smell?"

Crispin's witchlight flared around them, illuminating the black-rotted hatch to a coal cellar. The stench was appalling. Rot and fish, mud and smoke. Something green in the air too, something weirdly fragrant. Crispin sniffed. "Herbs?"

"Rosemary and thyme." Ned had a decided feeling of doom.

"Singing?"

"Oh yes."

"Bugger," Crispin said, and he'd never sounded more Cornish.

"Do I open the hatch? Try to keep it shut? What do we do?" He was shouting, he realised, because the damn voice was so damn loud in his head.

Crispin bent and put a finger to the sodden, ancient wood of the hatch, as if to write. The wooden doors swung wide at the touch, falling down into the hole beneath, and the smell rolled out over them like a fog.

Ned gagged violently, diaphragm lurching upward so he thought he might vomit. Crispin recoiled as though punched, clapping his hand over his mouth and nose.

It smelled like—well, Ned had never prised open the stone door to an ancient underground crypt to release centuries of rot and decay, wet flesh turning to earth and dry skin falling to dust, but now he had a fair idea what it would smell like if he did. The scent of herbs above the charnel stench made it, if anything, worse, like a corpse holding a posy of flowers. And the singing boomed out so loud that Ned staggered back, clamping his hands over his ears though he knew that was useless.

Then she'll be a true love of mine.

It stopped abruptly, leaving Ned with an absence of sound that should have been ringing in his ears and wasn't. It was so disorienting that he had to put a hand against the wall for support. "What's happening?"

"I don't know!"

"Oi!" It was a bellow from above and down the alley, a woman, judging by the voice, with her head stuck out the window. "What in the blooming heck are you doing down there? What's that light? What's that stink?"

"Get in the house!" Crispin yelled back, terror clear in his voice. "Lock the windows and don't come out!"

She didn't move. Ned took a deep breath and bellowed *"Get in!"* and she recoiled and slammed the window shut. "Uh," he added to Crispin, "why?"

"Call it a hunch." Crispin looked helplessly at him. "I don't want anyone getting hurt that we can avoid."

"You reckon someone's going to get hurt?"

"Don't you?"

Ned stared down into the dark space through the hatch. The witchlight pooled around the frame like liquid, but the darkness inside was untouched by it, as though it was sucking the light in. "Crispin?"

Crispin had his pencil and a scrap of paper out. He wrote a word with determination, and suddenly the brightness around them was like a patch of daytime in the night, but the doorway remained resolutely black.

"It, uh," Crispin said. "It's eating the light. I suppose we should…look inside?"

There was no way on God's earth Ned was going into anything that couldn't be lit and smelled like that. None. He turned to Crispin to make that very point, and they heard the crash.

It wasn't a huge crash like a wall falling in. Nothing like that. Just a regular, domestic, normal sort of breakage of the kind you might get if you smashed, for example, a stoneware jug.

"Oh no," Crispin said.

There was a second smash. Ned felt Crispin grab his arm, and then they were both stumbling backwards over the slippery cobbles, getting the hell away from the cellar, the smell, the thing that was breaking those witch bottles, and whatever the hell was going to happen.

"Any idea what that was?" Ned asked, as Crispin scrabbled for paper, dropping to one knee.

"No." It was a grunt of strain. Crispin was clutching his pencil in a fist, as though forcing words onto the paper balanced on his thigh. His lips were drawn back with effort. "I'm trying—can't—hold it in. It's—coming."

CHAPTER ELEVEN

The thing came out of the hatch in a slow, tumbling movement.

It was—Crispin didn't know what it was. It was a collection of rubbish, of rags and pottery shards, bones and dust; broken glass and bricks and wood; a tangle of straw and string and matted hair. And all of that stuff was somehow being pulled together, knitting itself into a single cohesive shape. A human shape.

The thing moved forward and as it did, Crispin realised there were bits coming off the ground and sticking to it with the awful semi-alive movement of iron filings fleeing to a magnet. A stray crumpled paper, a handful of muck, London's filthy detritus adding itself to the humanoid thing that formed legs and arms as he watched. It stank unbelievably, like a physical assault, reeking of old smoke and stagnant water, grave dirt and foul air. Crispin was breathing through his mouth, but that was very little defence.

Ned gazed at the thing, his face a mask of bewilderment, fear, and horror. "Look at it. It's getting *realer*."

It was a man-shaped vortex of rubbish, a whirling accretion of things, but as the waste was sucked in, it seemed to be compressed into solidity. A rat sped up its side and vanished into its chest, near a fragment of pottery that bore half a bearded face.

"Freckles!" Ned shouted. "Do something!"

That was a big help. Crispin had no idea at all what to do.

"Get behind it!" he yelled. He hoped something that sounded strategic would work better than *Run away!* and it did. Ned skittered up the alley toward Upper Thames Street, away from the river. Crispin looked back at the thing that housed a warlock.

As a boy, an odd, lonely, isolated sort of boy, he had spent a lot of time wandering the open spaces of Cornwall. He'd lived up on the cliffs where clear streams ran, and he'd been particularly fond of searching for casemakers, the larvae of caddisflies. You'd see a little lump of sticks and tiny stones oddly wedged together on the river bed, and realise it was the home a grub had built for itself, bits of this and that stuck together with silk. Sometimes he'd picked them up as the flies were emerging. It had always been an odd feeling to realise the jumble of detritus hid a living thing that was building itself a body.

The creature he faced—the spirit of John Kibble?—was a solid mass of rubbish, like a statue formed of the street's discards, but its eyes were alive and they were fixed on him. Its face shifted, a piece of crumpled rag stretching like a mouth, and it let out a rhythmic rattling sound, as though it had been shaken and jangled together. The cadence was rather like a laugh.

Crispin knew he should be doing something, had to act, but he couldn't seem to move. His mind was mired in the monstrosity in front of him. It was so old and so wrong. It smelled so bad.

The thing, the caddis, tipped its rag-and-bone head to one side, a shockingly human movement, and lifted an arm to Crispin. Rusty iron nails and a jagged splinter of wood stuck out for fingers, with what appeared to be a dead mouse for the thumb. He stared, frozen, as the limb extended towards him.

Something hit him so hard from the side that it knocked his breath out. He went flying down the alley, towards the river, tumbling to the filthy ground with a teeth-jarring impact, and lost any remaining air in his lungs as a heavy weight thudded on top of him.

"Freckles!" Ned yelled in his face. "Wake up!"

Crispin gasped for air. Ned scrabbled to a crouch. "Don't just lie there. What *is* it?"

Crispin looked up the alley, seeing the dark shape against the faintly lighter opening to Lower Thames Street. He couldn't tell if the thing was watching him or not.

"It's a caddis, I think. A warlock caddis. It's alive, and it's built itself a body to grow in while it gets stronger."

"It's evil," Ned said. "Isn't it? It's really bad. And it—" He scrubbed at his ear. "It's singing, but it's whispering too. Can you hear it whispering?"

"What's it saying?"

"I don't—" Ned's face convulsed. "No. I don't want to hear it. Freckles, it's *talking* to me!"

"I'll stop it," Crispin said, with far more certainty than he felt. "It's all right." He reached into his pocket as he spoke. "I can… Oh God. Oh my God!"

"What?" Ned demanded. He sounded closer to panic than Crispin had ever known him.

Crispin scrabbled in his inside pocket in case the pen had somehow escaped his touch or fallen down a hole in the lining, but he knew it hadn't. "My pen. I've dropped my pen!"

"Oh my days." They both looked around frantically, and Ned was the one to shout "There!"

He pointed. Crispin followed the finger and saw it. Back a few yards, where Ned had collided with him, the blood pen lay on the cobbles, silver glittering in the moonlight.

It was, perhaps, halfway between them and the caddis, and around it the lighter scraps and rubbish were beginning to jump and twitch like leaves in autumn, as the dust-heap creature exerted its pull.

"Oh no," Crispin whispered. "I have to get it."

"Don't go near it," Ned said. "I mean, you can do without it, right? You learned. You *said* you learned." His hand jerked to his ear, as though trying to block something out. "Shut up, you blasted— Get on and use a pencil!"

"It's not that. If that thing gets my pen…" Crispin's mouth was painfully dry. "It's my blood and bone, my power. It's *me*, and if the warlock eats it—" He stared at the little gleaming silver cylinder, and the growing shape beyond it, trapped in the awful dreamlike inevitability of catastrophe.

Fingers gripped his chin, pulling his face round. Ned kissed him hard, once, with force that pressed Crispin's lips against his teeth. "Love you," he rasped. Then he let Crispin go, almost with a push, and was up and running toward the caddis.

"*Ned!*" Crispin shrieked.

Ned bent low as he ran with a lunging, scooping motion that brought his hand to the ground, and the pen flew back towards Crispin. He leapt, wishing to catch it with mind and heart and every cell in his body, and he almost did. His fingers met the metal barrel and couldn't quite grip, and the pen bounced off his palm and went spinning away sideways into the darkness at the same moment that Ned, moving too fast to stop, tried to duck past the caddis.

It hit him.

It shouldn't have had so much strength. It was an accretion of rubbish held together by a dead man's will. But the mess of bone and clay and paper unfolded like a great machine's arm, lashed out with those iron claws, and hit Ned with a solid, fleshy thump that lifted him—so strong, so sturdy—off his feet like a rag doll and sent him flying into the shuttered door of a house.

Ned hit the ground, crumpled and boneless, and the caddis stalked towards him, a warlock in pursuit of a body.

Crispin flung himself to the side of the alley, witchlight flaring around him with reckless brightness, though there were windows opening above them at the noise. He needed his pen and couldn't see it, and he looked frantically back to the dark shape and saw it bent over Ned, its form flowing out and over, engulfing him. Consuming him.

"Ned!" Crispin shouted. "No, no, no! Look at *me*, you pile of filth!" He grabbed a half-rotted bit of timber and hurled it with all the strength and accuracy of which he was capable. It hit the caddis with a feeble thud, and stuck to it.

He needed the pen. It must have rolled when it hit the ground, hit the cobbles and bounced and rolled. It could be anywhere. He looked around with a terrified wild intensity, couldn't see it.

It had to be here somewhere. Crispin well knew that you could drop a thing in an empty room and it would vanish as though it had fallen through a hole in the world. His mother had always blamed buccas, mischievous pixies who stole your dropped coin or single sock. She'd used to cry, *Bucca, bring it back!* when she'd put her knitting needle down right there for just a moment and it had gone.

"Bucca, bring it back," Crispin whispered under his breath. "Bucca, please please please, where is it…"

There. A silver glint in the slime. He flung himself to his knees, grabbing for it, and almost sobbed at the familiar carving under his finger ends. He wrenched the top off, looked up at the caddis as it bent over Ned, and wrote.

He had no paper. To hell with paper. He wrote on the filthy wet cobbles, in a single great savage scrawl of blood, *Dispergere*, and felt searing pain rip down his spine at the force of it.

The caddis jolted violently, its agglomerated body rippling under the attack. For a second Crispin thought it was actually going to come apart, and then it tightened once more, knitting itself back together, over Ned.

Dispergere, Crispin wrote again harder, so hard that he could feel the stones of the street resonate under his hand and the blood pen drag strength from the marrow of his bones. "Dispergere, you bastard heap of shit. Dispergere!"

There was a rattle as a shower of detritus fell from the caddis, and Crispin could feel the suction in his hand as the warlock dragged strength to itself. The dustheap shape solidified once more, but this time it turned, rising from Ned, with something terrifyingly malevolent in its featureless face. Its stench hit Crispin in a wave of filth he could feel tainting his skin, and it took a jerky stride towards him. He leapt up, legs horribly weak under him, and stumbled a few steps backwards.

"What the bloody hell is that?" demanded a voice from the other side of the street. "What's going on out here?"

"Get in and lock your door!" Crispin screamed at the man who stood in an open doorway with a lamp. "It'll kill you!"

The caddis turned. It didn't move fast, but it didn't have to; the man was frozen in stunned horror at the impossible thing confronting him. He stood, mouth open, quite unable to react as the caddis reached out.

The stone Crispin threw bounced off the top of the caddis's head. "A-barth an pla!" he yelled at the top of his voice. Stone-throwing was childish defiance, but it was all he had at this moment, and the accompanying curses came out in the language of childhood too. "Molleth Dyw warnas! Kawgh an Jowl y'th vin!"

Perhaps the caddis understood Cornish and took offence, because it lurched back in its tracks and swung to face him once more. The man, released from his paralysis, took the opportunity to slam his door shut with force.

"Everyone stay indoors!" Crispin shouted at anyone who might be watching or listening. "You, John Kibble, kans mil molleth warnas!" He stepped backwards at the same time, with no idea what he was doing except leading the caddis away from Ned, from people. He glanced over his shoulder so he didn't trip, and his heart plummeted as he realised it was the deadest of dead ends. Crown & Horseshoe Wharf led down to nothing but its jetty, a black path jutting out into the

Thames. The river's usual grudging, sluggish swell was replaced by a moonlit sparkle, and a smell of salt as the sea drove up the great estuary and splashed over the planks of the dock. The water was as high as he'd ever seen it. A spring tide, probably, as moon and planets aligned to drag the waters up. No wonder Dr. Sweet had wanted to make his sacrifice tonight.

Tell her to find me an acre of land,
Between the salt water and the sea strand...

"Scarborough Fair." Crispin didn't know if he was picking it up somehow from singing he couldn't hear, or if the song had come into his head from Ned's words, but it gave him, if not an idea, a possibility. He ran further back, out onto the jetty. A wave splashed over the planks and his feet, soaking shoes and trouser legs.

"Hoi!" he shouted at the caddis. It was moving slowly, too slowly, and he couldn't let it turn back to Ned. He was not waste for its picking. "Dust-man, John Kibble! Come and get me! Ken dhe oela hwi a's bydh!" He waved the pen, then dropped to his knees and wrote *Dispergere* again, not so hard this time, still enough to make it shake. Keep it interested.

The caddis stepped onto the jetty, over the river.

Crispin scurried hastily backwards, right to the far end of the jetty, and knelt on the wood. He took one deep breath and another, pulling his strength and senses together. Not only the senses of a graphomancer, not just what Dr. Sweet had taught him, but the senses of a Cornish lad who'd grown up with the sea in his blood, who breathed and heard and felt its swell.

He shut his eyes and drew a shape that felt right to his hand, directly onto the planks. A spiral looping over the ground, getting larger, winding up the potential. He felt the suction in his own body, as well as the blood draining from his head, and steadied himself with his other hand as he drew it tighter and higher and harder and tenser with everything he had left in him, building, building—

He opened his eyes and looked up into a face of rag and bone, with a rat's nose poking outward, not a yard away from him. The caddis lifted its arm, and the rusty nails glinted death in the moonlight.

"Re'm fydh," Crispin whispered like a prayer, lifted his pen, and let everything he held snap free.

The wave hit the jetty like a giant's fist. It was the whole great force of the Thames at spring tide, and its pent-up force shook supports that had stood against storms for centuries. Crispin had just time to see the wall of water shatter the agglomerated man into a million tiny parts before he was swept off too, and his world became nothing but a freezing maelstrom without up or down or stop.

He shut his eyes and his airways tight, and concentrated on not panicking. This wasn't a storm but a single wave, and if he could hold his breath he'd get through it. He rode out the rush, letting himself be tumbled through the water as he had a thousand times as a boy playing in the surf at home. He just had to keep control of his burning lungs and wait it out.

His back hit something; he bounced off, felt himself swept again, and managed to hook a leg around whatever he'd hit. It was a thick, rough wooden strut. That meant he'd been swept along to the jetty of Rutland Wharf, and if he could hang on long enough to work out which way was up, there would be air.

He risked opening his eyes and saw only a stinging grey-brown fog of silt, but at least it was lighter one way than the other. He hauled himself in that direction, following the moonlight with his lungs aching and the wood abrading his hands, and broke through the turbulent water with a gasp.

The river was so high he'd barely need to haul himself up at all to roll onto the jetty, but even that effort seemed impossible. It was painfully cold in the water, sapping the strength from his bones, and God knew how much of his blood the pen had drained to command the tide, but it felt like a lot more than he'd had to spare. He clung to the jetty support, for lack of strength to do anything else, and in front of him saw flotsam bobbing. A piece of wood here, a rag there…

They came together, and held.

Crispin blinked water out of his bleary eyes and tried to focus. There was stuff floating all around him, little islands of rubbish forming on the waves, and they were drifting together as if pulled.

He didn't even notice getting onto the jetty in the sheer blinding terror of that realisation. He crawled on all fours until he had the strength to get upright, too afraid to wait, and then he ran, staggering and shivering, with his sodden clothes unbearably heavy around him; ran like hell, making little panting noises of exhaustion and terror because he'd lost his pen again, this time in the Thames for good, and his one idea hadn't bloody *worked*.

Along the slippery planks to the solid ground of Rutland Wharf, up the alley and across and back down Crown & Horseshoe Wharf, to where a body lay huddled on the filthy ground. Ned, curled in a ball with his arms wrapped around his head.

Not dead. He couldn't be dead.

"Ned!" Crispin stumbled to his knees and put a dripping hand to his shoulder. "Ned, are you all right? Talk to me!"

Ned's arm shifted slightly. He peered up with one eye, which widened. "Freckles?" His voice was harsh and strained, and too loud.

"Did it hurt you?" Crispin grabbed his arms, trying to uncurl him from his foetal ball. "Ned, what happened?"

"It's so loud," Ned said, his voice pitched as though he were talking over noise. "Can't think. Can you hear it?"

"No," Crispin whispered, staring at him. "I can't. Can you hear me?"

"Yeah." Ned blinked at him, with a look of frightened confusion that was utterly wrong on his face. "I can hear you talk quiet, *and* I can hear it sing, and I can hear—God help me—"

"What? What can you hear?"

"Everything!" Ned's hands jerked, as though he wanted to put them over his ears and had to stop himself. "It's not real. It's *not*."

"Well, it might be," Crispin said miserably. "Can you sit up?"

He dragged, and Ned pushed, and they got him sitting up. No blood, Crispin noted with relief. "Are you hurt?"

"Nothing broken," Ned said, which Crispin was sure meant, *I'm in agony*. "Hit the wall. Oh my days."

"What happened?" Crispin asked, dreading the answer.

"Don't know. That thing touched me. Not just the bits of dirt, either. There was some kind of…I don't know. Something in the air. I breathed it, I could *feel* I was breathing it, like a pea-souper, all thick and sticky and filthy, and—" He scrubbed a hand over his face, leaving a smear of grime. "It got into me. I can't explain it. It was like it was wrapping itself round my eyeballs and in my lungs and my ears, and I couldn't even scream, and suddenly everything was so bloody loud and it *won't stop*." His fingers closed urgently around Crispin's. "And then there was this pain, and the thing went away." He gave Crispin a bewildered look. "It got off me and went away and left me lying there. I thought I was going to die, and it just let *go*."

"That was me," Crispin said, with a certain amount of pride. "I lured it off."

Ned wasn't listening. His shoulders were dreadfully hunched. "Then there was a noise like about a hundred draycarts going by at once, like the whole city was going to shake apart. And it screamed." His face convulsed with remembered pain. "Oh my days, Freckles. That scream."

"I hit it with a wave, in the river. Smashed it to bits."

"You did? Is that why you're wet?" Ned blinked, understanding dawning in his clouded eyes. "Hang on, you killed it? But if it's dead— What did it do to me? What am I hearing? Why ain't it stopped?"

Crispin would have quite liked to be sick, or cry, but he didn't have time. He shot a glance down at the river before looking back to his lover. "I'm so sorry, Ned, and we'll try to fix whatever's happened to you, I promise, but the thing is, it's putting itself back together in the water *right now*."

"What?" Ned jerked to look around. "Bloody hell."

"We've got to run."

"Where to?"

That was the question. Crispin couldn't think of where to go. "We have to get help. Someone powerful. If I could find Mrs. Baron Shaw or Mr. Maupert…" Both of whom would be at home at this hour, and he had no idea where they lived. "Or the Golds. Dr. Gold's surgery is on Devonshire Street. If we go there, Mrs. Gold will—"

"Whoa there, wait." Ned's brows contracted. "That's miles. We can't leave that thing here and wander off. What if it tries to eat someone else?"

"There's nothing we can do. I've lost my pen. For good, this time. I was holding it when the wave hit me, and I dropped it in the Thames."

"Well, fuck," Ned said, which Crispin thought might have been the first time he'd heard him really swear. "Fuck. But—"

"I can't do anything! I hit it with a *wave* and that didn't work! How the devil do I destroy it if it can stand up to a wave?"

Ned's fingers tightened again. "All right, calm down. How long do you reckon till it's back together?"

They both looked at the river. There were just a few shapes floating on it now, large, dark, and moving steadily together.

"Not long," Crispin said.

"No. Right." Ned inhaled, deep and deliberate. "What was that thing playing at with me?"

"I think it was trying to take you over. Use your body."

"Like Marleigh wanted to use yours? Is that why I'm hearing all this stuff?"

"I don't know. Sorry."

"What happens when it gets a body?"

Crispin opened his hands helplessly. "Nothing good to the person. Other than that…" He imagined a two-centuries-dead vengeful spirit in an anonymous body, stalking the shadowed streets. "Oh Lord."

"We got to do something," Ned said. "And I don't mean bugger off, either. Can you shut this end of the street, like Sweet trapped me in the room?"

"There's people in the houses. I'd trap them in here with it."

"Right, no, blast. Set fire to it?"

"The body doesn't matter, that's why it came apart and didn't die. We need to get at its soul. Except I don't know how."

Crispin glanced at the river again. The dark shape that floated was one solid mass now, and it was very close to the edge of the wharf.

"All right then," Ned said. "You're not going to like this, but I got no other ideas."

"What?"

"That painter, the one caused all the trouble. The one who trapped people with his drawings and ripped them up. Could you do that to it? To its soul?"

"But—" Crispin's mouth moved as he assimilated the idea. "That's not allowed. It's not *lawful*."

"Do we care?"

Crispin cared. Other people would care, intensely, and that would be that for his future, his acceptance, his chance of making something of himself. He might as well tattoo *warlock* across his head if he returned to the justiciary with this news. *I killed a monster, because I'm a monster too!*

But Ned was flinching from sounds he shouldn't be able to hear because of what the caddis had done to him, with that terrible strain on his face. He would not let that happen to someone else, and if Crispin did, he knew all too well what Ned would think.

Crispin's awkwardly accommodated lives were splitting apart at last, with Ned on one side and magic on the other, and as he stared down the diverging paths of two futures, he discovered that the choice wasn't difficult at all.

"I'll do my best," he said. "Got any paper?"

Ned fished out a couple of folded sheets. Crispin patted his pockets in a sudden panic that he'd lost his pencil in the water too, but it was there.

Ned was looking down at the river. "Soon would be good. It's started singing again. Scarborough bloody Fair. It likes that song. Oh blast."

"What?" Crispin was intent on the paper, still uselessly blank, trying to think.

"It's started climbing out. Getting onto the wharf. Hurry."

"I don't know what I'm doing," Crispin said through his teeth. "I need time."

"Right. Time." Ned's voice had that consciously calm, refusing-to-panic note. "Uh, so, I could distract it? Or— Whoa, whoa, hang on. That spell. That was you, right? Can't you do that again?"

"What spell?"

"When it got off me. It was singing, and you shouted that stuff. You confused it."

"That wasn't a spell. I was swearing."

"Eh? It wasn't English."

"Cornish. I need to concentrate."

"Oi." Ned grabbed his shoulder. "*Listen.* It was singing, and you yelled that stuff, whatever it was, and that scrambled it up like eggs. Like if someone was singing and you started playing a different tune. Got right under its skin. Don't you see? *That's* what we got to do."

"But I can't swear at it and draw at the same time!"

"No," Ned said. "So—" He yanked Crispin over for a swift kiss, looking deep into his eyes, moonlit and intent. "I love you, Freckles. So much. But it's got on the quay, so I'm off to see about a bit of bad language, and you do some pictures, all right?"

"Ned!" Crispin yelped, but he was already on his feet, stepping away, towards the caddis.

He'd made his choice because he believed in Crispin, believed he'd have an answer. And that was terrifying because Crispin had no idea how to do this. He needed to draw the essence of the thing, he knew that much, but how could you draw what you couldn't see, something that was just ash and bone and stolen life?

Crispin looked hopelessly at the paper. If he only knew anything about what was making the caddis live…

Ned was shouting at it, in quite startling terms. Apparently his usual restraint in profanity wasn't for lack of ability. Crispin hoped everyone had their windows shut.

He let his hand move. A couple of lines to suggest Dr. Sweet's kindly eyes. A few more to give an impression of Voake's dull ones, since Voake was in there somewhere, he was sure, but that was all he knew…

"Freckles!" Ned bellowed. "Swearing's not working!"

Crispin glanced up. The dripping caddis was halfway along the wharf, moving towards him, Ned backing up in front of it. He wanted to scream at him to run away, but that wasn't what they were doing here. "I need more time!"

Ned was silent for a couple of seconds, and then he began to sing. He had a marvellous voice, deep and rich, and not at all suited to the song he belted out now, which was an outrageous music-hall sensation.

"I'll sing of Hildebrand Montrose,
(his proper name is Charlie.)
He speaks as tho' with cold in his 'dose',
bad French he tries to parly."

They'd seen it performed a couple of months back and laughed themselves silly at the performer's campish style. Ned occasionally broke into the infectious chorus as he worked, adopting a la-di-da voice because when you were a big, strong, manly sort of man, you could get away with that. Crispin wouldn't have dared.

"His hair is in barber's ringlets,
his eyes are made up dark,
He walks upon his uppers
while strolling in the park..."

Crispin risked a look up to see that the caddis had slowed. It was unquestionably struggling in the face of the absurd song, and at the same time, Crispin felt he had something. His pencil flew. A swift scrawl to suggest rosemary—that's for remembrance—parsley, sage, and thyme, nothing detailed, but it was representation that mattered here. He was drawing the malevolence of it, the blank callousness, the cruel, merciless essence of a warlock who used other people without care and discarded them without regret...

Ned roared out the refrain.

"Au revoir, ta, ta! you'll hear him say,
To the Marchioness Clerkenwell,
While bidding her good-day..."

Crispin glanced up again. The caddis was fighting against the song, coming closer now, a great dripping mass of rubbish and stink, with malevolence radiating from it, and there was an awful forced belligerence in Ned's deep, strong, resonant voice—

Resonance. That was it.

"I'll strike you with a feather," Ned sang with a snarl in his voice that made it sound remarkably like a genuine threat.

"I'll stab you with a rose,
For the darling of the ladies,
Is Hildebrand Montrose."

"Keep singing!" Crispin shouted at him, and then, as his pencil flew, he joined in. Or rather, he didn't.

"His scarf, unlike himself, is green, his gloves, no kid, are yaller..." Ned sang, and Crispin came in at the same time, as loud as he could, in a different tune and words he could have sung in his sleep.

"A good sword and a trusty hand!

A merry heart and true!
King James's men shall understand
What Cornish lads can do!"

On the page, a tangle of herbs trapped the eyes of the dead men he knew and shaded a suggestion of the dead he didn't, and around it he sketched the Bellarmine jug as though all of it was set in stoneware.

Ned's baritone boomed out the frivolous bit of music hall:

"His washed-out pants are well strapped down,
He carries a fake umbrella..."

Crispin's light, high tenor warbled the martial 'Song of the Western Men':

"Here's twenty thousand Cornish men
Will know the reason why!"

God alone knew what it must sound like to the people in the houses around, let alone to the caddis; it was confusing the hell out of Crispin. Ned had his hands clamped over his ears and the sinews were standing out on his neck, but he kept singing even as he backed slowly towards Crispin because the caddis was still coming on. It was slowed, shaking and staggering, but it wasn't stopping, and it was no more than ten feet away.

Crispin gripped the pencil, going over the lines. Writing the warlock onto the paper, writing his bottled malevolence and stolen life—

"I'll strike you with a feather," Ned sang, jumping back to stand by Crispin's shoulder. *"I'll stab you with a rose—"* A moon-shadow fell over the paper. "Freckles!"

Crispin looked up at the half-living man-shaped thing that loomed over him, and ripped his drawing in half.

It hurt. It hurt extraordinarily, so much that he couldn't breathe, and he had a single terrifying second where he thought that he had tangled himself in his own web. Above him the caddis loomed, its waste-formed face staring blankly down, its arm raised.

Its hand fell off. It dropped to the ground in a shower of rusty nails, dust and splinters that bounced off the cobbles, spraying into Crispin's face. The caddis made a rattling noise. It shook.

Ned crashed to the floor as though his tendons had been cut, the heels of his hands pressed to his ears.

Crispin tore the paper again, and again, feeling the internal wrench every time. A shower of detritus rained from the caddis as it lost coherency, and Crispin saw a great brown rat flee down its leg and away.

"Make it shut up!" Ned screamed. He was thrashing like a fish in a net, spasming in pain. The caddis was *hurting* him.

Crispin looked up at the caddis, the warlock, the spirit desperately striving to live, and he took one of the pieces of torn paper and wrote, in simple English, *Die*.

There was a rattling crash as a lot of rubbish that had been precipitously balanced in a humanoid shape fell to the cobbles, and then, at last, silence.

Crispin knelt, breathing hard. He had to go to Ned, but he felt as though he were made out of hollow straws and the slightest movement would make the fragile structure collapse. He wanted to be sick, but his muscles couldn't find the strength. His hand was numb to the wrist, and he stared at it, not quite sure if it even belonged to him any more. He was still staring when he passed out.

CHAPTER TWELVE

By the next afternoon, after spending the entire day in a cell, Ned wasn't sure if he was more angry, afraid, or bored.

He'd woken up in this little windowless, whitewashed room with a bed, a chair, a chamber pot. A nasty-faced character with a badly broken nose had brought him a pitcher and bowl and a set of clean clothes, which was a relief, but he'd not even reacted to Ned's questions, let alone answered them. There'd been a doctor after, a Jewish-looking chap who had touched Ned's ears, asked a series of questions, muttered under his breath. He'd spent a good hour there, testing what sounds Ned could hear, both real ones and the other kind, and he'd spoken like a civil man, though a harried one, but he'd refused to answer any of Ned's questions: *Where am I? Where's Crispin? Who are you people?*

He reckoned he could answer at least two of those himself, mind. He could hear it: something like the strange muted hum that had been coming off Crispin, but a whole lot of them, a chorus of different frequencies that rose and fell, ebbed and flowed. That would be magic. He was being kept in Crispin's Council place, and he could hear magic. The warlock was dead and gone, again, but he could still bloody hear bloody *magic*.

Ned was very, very unhappy about that, and he was none too pleased about being held in a cell without trial or warrant or explanation either. At least they gave him lunch.

He was pretty thoroughly narked by the time the door opened to reveal a man so short Ned thought for a second he must be a messenger boy.

"Mr. Hall," the chap said. "I'm Stephen Day, senior justiciar. Sorry for the delay."

"Delay? I've been here all day. What time is it?"

"Nearly four." Day had messy dark-red hair flopping into his peculiar amber eyes and a generally dishevelled look. "There's been quite a lot to sort out. I've some questions to ask."

"So've I," Ned said firmly. "Where's Crispin Tredarloe?"

"Safe and well," Day said. "Unlike Dr. Sweet, who is quite outstandingly dead. Mr. Hall, you should be aware that Mr. Tredarloe is in deep trouble right now."

"What? He killed a monster! Sweet was a murderer!"

"So Tredarloe tells us. What we actually have to go on is a tortured corpse, blood magic, a huge amount of power exerted in the open street, and clear evidence of more unlawful activity in one short space of time than I've seen since December."

It was only just turned April. "Is that bad?"

Day shrugged. "December was a low point. I need to know what happened yesterday, Mr. Hall, and I'd like you to tell me. I'd also like to verify you're telling the truth." He held up a hand. There was a gold ring on one finger, set with black and white stones, surprisingly flash for such a scruffy little tyke. Ned could hear a faint buzzing sound as his hand moved. "With your consent, I can do that easily. You don't have to consent, of course." He smiled. It wasn't very friendly. "Not if you have anything to hide."

"Are you talking about doing magic on me?"

"Yes," Day said. "Which I have both the ability and the authority to do, whether you like it or not. Currently, I'm asking, but I won't be doing that for long. I don't have time for games."

"I don't have the inclination," Ned said. "Thing is, you're justiciary, that's magician police, right? I'm not a magician."

"Mmm. Nevertheless, I need you to talk to me, Mr. Hall, because there is circumstantial evidence and a body of opinion that Tredarloe is a warlock, a necromancer, and a murderer, and you're the only witness I have to sort this out. Will we do this the easy way or not?"

Ned exhaled hard. "I'll tell you the truth and you can check that. But no making me do stuff, and no making me say things I don't want. I've had about as much as I can stomach of your lot, Crispin excepted, and I'm not inclined to trust you as far as I can throw you. No offence."

"None taken," Day said. "I feel the same way myself, except that I don't trust Tredarloe either. All right, this will feel a little odd." He touched the back of Ned's hand.

"Ow! What the—"

"Only me. Very well, Mr. Hall. Tell me all about it."

So Ned talked. He went from the beginning—telling the truth that Crispin had been round his gaff when the burning happened, and not making up a reason why because he wasn't going to risk a lie to this odd little bloke with his electric fingers and yellow eyes. He told about Janossi, and his own investigations, which Day seemed to want to know a lot about, and Sweet kidnapping him, and the witch bottle they'd made.

Day stopped him there. "You were communicating across a distance by writing?"

"It was because of Crispin's pen," Ned said. "The special one."

"The blood pen. Why did you have that?"

"I was looking after it for him."

"I see. And you could use it?"

"Sort of," Ned said. "I could write with it, but not do magic."

"Mmm. Whose blood did it use?"

"Mine, I reckon. Hurt like nobody's business." He indicated the back of his neck. Day raised a brow for permission and touched a buzzing forefinger to the top of his spine. Ned twitched.

"Yes, I see. That's…interesting. Go on."

He went on—the search for the bottles, finding Sweet drowning, the thing from the cellar.

"And Crispin had dropped his pen," he finished up. "So I went and got it and chucked it to him, but the blasted creature swiped me." He indicated his side, which was painfully bruised.

"Did you not think it might attack you when you went to retrieve the pen?"

"Had a fair idea it'd rip my head off," Ned said bluntly. "But Crispin needed the pen. Well, I thought he did. Turns out he didn't."

"No," Day said. "It appears he was perfectly able to snuff out a life simply by drawing it."

"Is he going to get in trouble for that?"

"I expect so."

"Well he shouldn't." Ned found, suddenly, that he was quite extraordinarily angry. "He's worked his arse off trying to do the right thing. Sweet was going to kill me, and Crispin's first thought was still to stop that witch bottle before it blew up. Fellow'd be alive now if it wasn't for those jugs, and Crispin had nothing to do with that. He didn't even want to write that warlock thing dead, he only did it because it was going to kill people. Your chap Sweet was the necrowhatsit here; not one of you justiciary people saw a triple murderer under your noses, to say nothing of a dead warlock come back just down the road; and you're trying to blame *Crispin*?" He took a much-needed breath. "He's the only worthwhile one of you people I've met, and that's the truth. What's so funny?"

"I was thinking you really ought to meet a friend of mine," Day said. "You'd get on like a house on fire. All right, your point is noted. Carry on, Mr. Hall."

Ned didn't much want to tell the next bit, the warlock thing's attack on him. He felt dirty, and weak, and ashamed, even, which was damn stupid. But he told it anyway, and the vague bits he could recall of what Crispin had done with the wave.

"But he'd lost his pen in the water, and I…wasn't feeling too chipper." He realised he was rubbing at his ear and brought his hand away, somewhat self-consciously. "So we put our heads together. It was my idea for Crispin to draw it and rip the paper up. He wanted to go and get someone, one of your lot, but we didn't reckon we had time."

"Because?"

"Because it would have killed people," Ned said. "You not listening? I *told* you about that thing. It would have had me if Crispin hadn't stopped it, no question."

"I understand that," Day said. "I don't understand how a waste-paper trader and a shambles of a half-trained practitioner felt qualified to confront a revenant of significant power. It's not as though either of you knew what you were doing."

Ned had to gasp for breath at that. "Go fry your face," he managed, when he could control his tongue. "We bloody well did it, didn't we? I worked out how to slow it down, waste-man or not. Crispin killed it without even having his pen. There wasn't a soul hurt, and you're sat there high-and-mighty saying we did it wrong? What, we should have twiddled our thumbs and waited for your lot to turn up? What would you have done in my place?"

"How did you slow it down?" Day asked, unmoved.

"Sang at it," Ned said, still bristling with annoyance.

"Sang?"

"It kept singing 'Scarborough Fair' in my head, right from the start. I sang back at it the first night and that shut it up for a bit. Then, last night, Crispin yelled at it in this singsong foreign, Cornish, and that confused it, I could hear. Sort of interfered with what it was doing, don't ask me why. So I sang at it."

"And you deduced that for yourself?"

Ned gave him a look. "Any reason I shouldn't have?"

Day shrugged. "I've seen brave men in these situations panic to the point they forget how doors work. What did you sing?"

Ned glowered. "Hildebrand Montrose."

Day clamped his lips together, but there was no hiding the laugh in his eyes. "I see," he said, slightly shakily. "That must have been striking. Then what?"

"Crispin tore up the paper. It screamed." He felt himself shudder at the memory of that screaming, like a saw on rusty iron, screeching and ripping through his head so that every nerve and sinew felt weak and slack. "And I don't remember anything more till I woke up here."

Day nodded and lifted his prickling fingers away. "Thank you, Mr. Hall. I'll need you to come with me now."

"Where to?"

"The Council of Practitioners. There is going to be a discussion about what to do with you and Tredarloe, and—"

"Hold your horses," Ned said. "I'm not a magician."

"Practitioner. Get used to the word, please."

"I don't have to. I'm not under your authority, Mr. Day, and I don't answer to your Council."

"That remains to be seen." Day pulled out a watch and squinted at it. "Come on, Mr. Hall. We don't want to be late."

Day brought him through a set of corridors that changed from shabby whitewash to grand panelling, and then to a large hall hung with gilt-framed paintings. There was an impressive set of doors at one end and, standing by them, the justiciar Janossi, and Crispin.

He looked round as Ned approached. A flash of joy lit his face and disappeared almost at once. "Ned? What are you doing, Mr. Day?"

"You're both going to have to answer questions," Day said. "Bring them in when we give the word, Joss, I'm going to…" He waved a hand vaguely and went through the great doors, leaving Ned and Crispin staring at each other.

"Are you all right?" they said together.

"Fine," Ned said, going first. "Bit sore, no bones broken. The hearing business hasn't gone away."

"Oh no." Crispin's hand went to his mouth. He was obviously exhausted, wan and worn, with circles under his eyes so dark that he looked like he'd been punched. "I'm sorry. Is it bad?"

It wasn't bad at all right now, in fact, just a faint hum. Ned could live with that as part of London's endless uproar. "Fine as long as nobody starts screaming. What about you?"

Crispin made a face. "Not very good. In a bit of trouble, I think. I shouldn't really have done a lot of the things I did."

"Like you had a choice," Ned said. "What were you going to do, let it kill people? Anyway, the drawing was my idea and so I told that fellow."

"I doubt the Council will think much of that," Janossi observed.

Ned turned on him. "Look, sunshine, you had your chance to stop this and you missed it. If you're planning to get at Crispin for clearing up your mess, take a walk."

"*Ned*," Crispin said, in something of a wail.

"Don't be a chump. This is a stitch-up, and I don't see any reason to be civil about it." The misery in Crispin's face was unbearable. Ned clapped him on the arm, since he couldn't hold him properly. "Come on, chin up. You're better than the lot of 'em."

"I don't feel it. I'm scared, and I don't want—" He cut that off abruptly, shut his eyes for a second, and took a deep breath. "Well. It's how it is. And I really wish you weren't being dragged into this with me, but I'm glad you're here. If that makes sense."

"Me too, mate." Ned met Crispin's eyes, knowing he'd understand what was being said. "Me too."

"So much," Crispin responded, a real smile dawning, and if they couldn't kiss here in this stupid poncy hall, well, that was the next best thing.

A shout came from behind the double doors. Janossi opened one and ushered them in.

The room they entered was large and mostly empty, a big meeting space with a long half-moon table taking up the end of the room. There was a row of men sitting at it, with a woman in the middle looking at them over her spectacles with a resigned expression. At the far end of the table, after a meaningful-looking gap, sat Day. Mrs. Gold, the justiciar he'd met back in summer, was next to him, a bit back from the table to accommodate her huge belly. A big burly red-faced sort who resembled a butcher sat at the end.

"Well, Tredarloe," said the woman in the middle of the table, somewhat wearily. "As if we needed more trouble."

"All of you know Tredarloe, I think," Mrs. Gold said. "The other one's Edward Hall, a flit who seems to have had a minor hearing talent substantially enhanced by his encounter with the revenant. As such, Mr. Hall, you're coming under our jurisdiction for last night's escapade. Councillors on the table today are Mr. Maupert, Mr. Felworthy, Mrs. Baron Shaw, chair, and Mr. Harrington. For the justiciary, this is Mr. Macready, I'm Mrs. Gold, if you recall, and you've met Mr. Day. That makes up your panel of seven, as required to address charges of torture, murder, warlockry, necromancy, causing death by unlawful practice, reckless endangerment, and public displays of practice."

"Charges by who?" Ned demanded. "We didn't do any of that!"

Crispin coughed. "Well, we did some."

"And it all happened," Mrs. Gold said. "I appreciate your indignation, Mr. Hall, but I'm sure you see that we need to understand *why* it happened. We cannot have practitioners running around killing people."

"Your Dr. Sweet—"

"Including him," Mrs. Baron Shaw said. "Not that he's running around any more, and heaven knows how we'll explain *that* to All Souls. Go on, Mrs. Gold."

She nodded. "Stephen has Mr. Hall's account of the business, I have Tredarloe's. Tredarloe, start from the beginning, tell it again, leave nothing out, and don't diverge from the truth."

Crispin launched into the tale once more. Ned looked around, baffled. This wasn't like any legal proceeding he'd heard of, with no counsel and no dock. No prosecution, either. He'd assumed there'd be accusations and speeches and twisting of the facts, but it was nothing but silent people listening intently.

Very intently. Day was resting his small chin on steepled fingers, and his yellow eyes were fixed on Ned. Everyone else was watching Crispin, and Ned could hear a gentle humming in the air.

Crispin got to the bit about Ned's investigations, and Mrs. Baron Shaw lifted a hand. "We'll have that from Mr. Hall, please."

Every set of eyes switched to Ned, except Mrs. Gold's. She stayed watching Crispin like a cat.

Ned cleared his throat and told what he'd deduced and discovered, and he was really sure there was magic being done at that point, or at least floating around the room. The three justiciars seemed to listen with remarkable attention, and when he'd finished both Day and Mrs. Gold flicked looks that Ned couldn't interpret at the third justiciar, Macready.

Crispin took over the story again and went on until the bit where Sweet kidnapped Ned. They had to tell all that twice, once from each perspective, and Ned didn't like the quality of the silence as they spoke. Crispin went on till the warlock's attack, then Ned had to go over what had happened to him *again*, this time to all these people, and that was a humiliation he could have done without. Day's eyes on him might have been sympathetic, or they might not.

At last, after endless talking, they were done. There was a longish pause, and Mrs. Baron Shaw said, "Questions?"

Mr. Felworthy, a thin, niggly sort of fellow with a pointed nose, raised a finger. "Tredarloe claims he asked Mrs. Gold for assistance and was told no justiciars were available. Why not?"

"You know perfectly well why not," Mrs. Gold said.

"Yes, I do. Because the justiciary were concerned with avenging an injury to one of their own rather than the maintenance of proper order."

"Because," Day said loudly, "we have still not got the extra manpower promised in December, and since Saint and I are both leaving by the end of the month—"

"*Because*," Mr. Harrington said over him, "you are being so damned dilatory about recruiting—"

"Can we kindly keep this discussion for another time!" Mrs. Baron Shaw said, with startling volume, as everyone started talking at once. "Thank you. *Relevant* questions, please."

"I've one," Day said. "What on earth was Sweet playing at, Tredarloe? Do you have any idea what he was trying to achieve?"

Crispin's eyes widened in alarm. "Uh, well—"

"I can answer that," Mrs. Gold said over him. "It appears Dr. Sweet had been interested in John Kibble, and his ability to control and absorb power, for a long time. He found one of the Bellarmine jugs in the All Souls collection, and retrieving the others seems to have been an academic interest that grew into an obsession. He discovered that they had been passed on until their significance was forgotten. They ended up in London, in the possession of an elderly lady—not a practitioner, no family. The house was cleared on her death, which I suppose is how the jugs ended up in various rag and bottle shops. Sweet made it his mission to track them down."

Everyone was looking at her. "May I ask how you know that?" Mrs. Baron Shaw enquired.

"Because he wrote a book about it."

"I beg your pardon?"

"A pamphlet, anyway." Mrs. Gold held up a slim booklet. "*The Curious History of an Oxfordshire Witch-Burning*. He published it last November. It gives the history and a lot of theorising about how one could track the jugs down, and more or less spells out his intention to retrieve the accursed things. He used resonance theory, apparently."

"Published," Day said. "Well, that's embarrassing."

"Resonance theory," Mrs. Gold repeated pointedly. "Comment, Mr. Maupert? I recall you saying you followed Dr. Sweet's work with close attention."

Mr. Maupert shifted in his seat. "I, uh, may have…I did read it, yes, but I'm quite sure his intentions weren't obvious at the time."

"With the benefit of hindsight, they're glaring," Mrs. Gold said. "Even more embarrassing is the fact that he wrote to us asking for a residency here a bare month after publishing the pamphlet. He came to London to track down these blasted jugs and we gave him office space to do it. And we also gave him Tredarloe."

All eyes switched back to Crispin. "Do you know why he wanted you?" Day asked.

"He said he thought I'd be of help in his work," Crispin said. "He wanted me to come to Oxford with him. He didn't say why, but he knew how to get my talent working, and I believed he was helping me. I'd probably have done anything he told me."

The angry shame in Crispin's voice grated on Ned's nerves. He shouldn't be the one ashamed by this. "You weren't to know. You should've been able to trust him."

"Yes, you should. But you couldn't, and we—I—put you right into his hands," Mrs. Gold said. "Sorry about that."

"Quite." Mrs. Baron Shaw looked at the justiciars over the top of her spectacles. "Perhaps the next time someone delivers their murderous intentions to us in printed and bound form, we could pay a little more attention."

Mr. Macready cleared his throat in a changing-the-subject sort of way. "Tredarloe. You accept the revenant posed a significant threat to life. You knew it was absorbing people and power. Did it cross your mind what would have happened if it had got you?"

Crispin looked completely blank. "Uh…"

"People felt that wave of yours a mile and a half away. You've got plenty of power, and when you deliberately put yourself in the way of a creature that could have fed off you, you risked a great deal more than yourself and your friend. That was irresponsible behaviour which could have had appalling consequences."

"Yeah," Ned said, since Crispin appeared speechless. "But it didn't, because he killed the warlock before it hurt anyone."

Macready's eyes narrowed. "That's not the point. If a creature of that type had absorbed Tredarloe's powers—"

"Which it didn't," Ned repeated. "If Crispin hadn't dealt with it, that thing would have killed people. There's already three dead over this. And that may not be the point to you gentlemen, because it's not your people would have took the brunt, but it looks like the point to me. So you can call what Crispin did irresponsible if you like, but we were *there*, dealing with it, and you justiciary weren't. If you don't like it, bloody well turn up and do the work yourself. Excuse my French, ma'am."

"Think no more of it," said Mrs. Baron Shaw graciously. "Nevertheless, it is relevant. *Did* you consider what would happen if it absorbed your powers, Mr. Tredarloe?"

"No," Crispin said miserably. "I didn't think of that at all. I just didn't want it to hurt anyone else. Sorry."

"I have a question," said the bloke identified as Mr. Maupert, a dried-up, miserable old stick, to Ned's mind, who had been looking daggers at Crispin for most of the hearing. "Tredarloe, you have admitted that you used first your illicit blood pen and then a particularly revolting form of murderous graphomancy. After seven months of remedial training, why were you unable to use any sort of sanctioned or acceptable power? Is it not the case that you have neither capacity nor will to learn other methods?"

Crispin looked wretched, guilty, and sweaty, and his voice was shaky as he answered, "I don't have the capacity. It's not lack of will,

I've tried my hardest, but I'm a graphomancer. I can't be anything else."

"No," Mr. Maupert said with cold precision. "That is what I have long feared. It is my view that there is nothing to be done with this young man. He resorts to blood magic and the worst kind of practice at the slightest need. It is quite unacceptable."

The slightest need? Ned drew in a deep breath to give his opinion of that, and heard, clear as a bell, the words right in his ear: *Quiet, now.*

He blinked, startled. Someone must have said that by unnatural means, but not one of the seven magicians opposite was looking at him.

"Your point is noted, Mr. Maupert," said Mrs. Baron Shaw. "Unless anyone has further questions, we'll consult. Janossi, take them to wait, and for heaven's sake feed Tredarloe before he collapses."

Janossi took them back to the not-quite-cell where Ned had been kept, and went off to get food. He left the door open. Ned glanced at it.

"Don't bother," Crispin said, taking a chair. "No point. They won't stop coming after me if we do run."

Ned sat as well. "What's going to happen?"

"No idea."

"What's the worst?"

Crispin made a face. "If they really thought I was dangerous, they'd do something to stop me. Prison, or…well, you hear about people who disappear and never come back, or people who get stopped from using their powers." He held his hands out, palms up, looking at the slim fingers. "They might stop me writing."

"No," Ned said. "They can't do that, can they?"

"They can. I don't know if they will. Mr. Maupert—"

"I meant to ask. What did you ever do to that old buzzard?"

"Wrecked his study," Crispin admitted. "And he couldn't teach me. And he's not very nice."

"Still that's no reason—"

Someone passed the door, stopped, and came to peer in. It was the unpleasant chap with the broken nose. "Tredarloe," he said in a tone that made Ned bristle. "In trouble *again*. They'll have you this time."

"You know," Crispin said, a little nervously but with determination, "I'm sure I could fix your nose."

That set the fellow on the back foot. "What?"

"Your nose. I could redraw it, I think. Only if you wanted, of course, but I'm happy to try."

The man's mouth opened and closed. He appeared bereft of words. "Is that a threat?" he demanded at last.

"No, it's an offer," Crispin said. "Of help. Let me know."

Janossi came up behind him with a laden tray. "Oh, not you. Go *away*, Waterford. Here, you two." He put the tray on the little table and stepped back. It was heaped with sandwiches and buns, with a pot of tea steaming at one side. "Get that down you. While I'm here, I wanted to say thank you."

"For what?" Ned asked.

"Dealing with a murderer and a warlock," Janossi said. "Nobody else is going to say it, believe me. But I heard what you two did, and to be quite honest, I don't give two hoots how you did it, as long as it got done. And I know you're listening out there, you pig-faced prat, and you can tell anyone I said so." That was with a malevolent look at, or through, the wall. "Anyway, good luck. The iced buns are the best."

Ned turned to look after him as he left. "You lot really are peculiar."

Crispin grunted agreement through half a bun. Ned sighed and poured the tea. "What's the ugly bloke's problem?"

"Waterford? I think he's quite unhappy," Crispin said. "So he's unpleasant, and then people are unpleasant to him, and so on. I thought I'd try being nice, just to see what happens."

Ned couldn't have stopped the smile spreading across his face if he'd wanted to. "You're something special, F—Crispin."

"Oh, well," Crispin said. "You're not so bad yourself."

They couldn't talk here, not properly. The door was open, there were any amount of peculiar people about who could stick their noses in by magical means, and they were in quite enough trouble already without being heard saying the big, important things. So Ned just leaned back and stretched out his legs so as to touch Crispin's foot with his own, and they sat in silence, with that little connection between them, and waited for judgement.

He was almost nodding off when Day came in, accompanied by Mrs. Gold.

"Gentlemen." Day shut the door and moved his hand with a sharp fizzing crackle that made Ned jump, and which Crispin clearly didn't hear. Doing something magic, Ned was sure. Both justiciars sat.

"What did they say?" Crispin asked, sitting forward. "I mean…is there a Council decision?"

"Council decision." Mrs. Gold rolled her eyes. "Oxymoron."

That seemed a bit harsh to Ned. Day said, "Thank you, Esther. There is a consensus of sorts, which I will tell you, I have argued for in strong terms. It's clear Mr. Tredarloe has a dangerous and intimidating talent that cannot simply be let loose. It seems evident that he can't or won't learn another method of practice, and he has demonstrated a remarkable obstinacy in pursuit of his goals." He looked directly at Crispin, who was going a bit pale. "If you had taken time to seek assistance from other, more experienced people, instead of haring off after Sweet on your own, it would be a different matter. As it is, there is only one thing I, or any of us, can think to do with you, Mr. Tredarloe."

Ned kept his breathing steady. Crispin licked his lips, evidently bracing himself.

Day said, "Justiciary."

There was a fractional silence. Crispin said, "What?"

"We want you in the justiciary. It's quite evidently where you belong."

"*What?*"

"Jus-tic-i-ary," said Mrs. Gold, enunciating clearly. "Was your hearing affected as well?"

Day sighed. "I do wish you'd give birth and have done. On the one hand, Tredarloe, we could use you. If you were the justiciary's graphomancer, if I had you—"

"You're leaving," Mrs. Gold pointed out, in the tone of one who had mentioned this before.

"If *Esther* had you in the corner sketching suspects while they were questioned, wouldn't that concentrate a few minds? When we let someone go on the promise of good behaviour, suppose we had you draw them, just to make sure? And then there's the writing. I cannot tell you how useful that could be. If I'd been able to contact Esther from a distance—with that business at Crane's house last year, Es, or in December—"

"Don't remind me," Mrs. Gold said. "Of course we need to find out if Tredarloe can do that with other people. Or help other people do it, if there's any way. Or—"

"Whoa, whoa," Ned said. "Hold your horses. All right, I see how Crispin's useful to you. But you said *on the one hand*, and we ain't heard the other one yet."

"Fair point." Day sat back. "On the other hand, then, we want you, Tredarloe, but you need us. Within the justiciary you'd have a framework, you'd have approval, you'd have people on your side. We can use your talents for the law, and that makes them lawful."

"Is that how it works?" Ned asked.

"More or less." Day contemplated Crispin, tilting his head. "The thing is, you're not normal. Extraordinary talents, bad beginnings, unsavoury associations. You're odd. —Settle down, Mr. Hall, I haven't finished. Because the thing about being odd is, it can *become* normal. Right now you're that peculiar chap with the pen who doesn't fit in, the possible warlock. In the justiciary, you would quickly become the justiciar who draws, as opposed to the short one, the flying one, or the bad-tempered one the size of a house."

"Oh, go to the devil," Mrs. Gold told him.

"People want to think they know who you are. Well, if you're a justiciar, that *is* who you are. You develop your talents, we use them, it becomes normal, you have a place to fit. Nobody thinks twice about you any more—you, Crispin Tredarloe, rather than you, justiciar." Day gave a twitch of a smile. "Some of us find it convenient not to be noticed."

A place to fit. That was what Crispin needed, no question. Ned couldn't quite believe his place would be in the law, but then Day wasn't his idea of a lawman either. Maybe you grew into it.

Crispin was clearly thinking along the same lines. "Um. I understand that. But... Look, Mr. Day, I'm just not like that."

"Not like a justiciar?" Day said. "No, very true, you're not. That's another reason I want you."

"Sorry?"

"You see, the justiciary needs an obstinate, pig-headed misfit," said Mrs. Gold. "And since Steph's leaving, there's a vacancy."

Day grinned. "Quite. We are in serious need of manpower, and yet I've been declining Macready's candidates precisely because they're Mac's. He's a good man, a good justiciar, but he's not imaginative, or empathetic, or fearful. We need hobnailed boots and intimidation sometimes, that goes without saying, but we need the other things too. I want justiciars whose first priority is to stop people getting hurt. Who *think*. Who aren't exactly like all the other people in charge. Who have the courage to go against what everyone else is telling them. Mac's a damned brave man, but he believes in authority, and if you do that, you end up just doing what you're told—"

"—and God forfend the justiciary should obey the Council," Mrs. Gold finished sardonically.

"Not slavishly. We can't," Day said. "Any more than the Council should obey us. If you start agreeing that people are right because of the position they hold rather than what they do with it, you end up Lord knows where. We *need* different, Tredarloe. We need uncertain. We need seeing other people's points of view, and wondering if you're right after all."

"Well, that's me," Crispin said.

"And we need people who can go through all that and still *act*," Day went on. "I'm asking you to make a decision, but it seems to me you made it yourself when you took on Dr. Sweet and his revenant. I think you have talent, determination, and heart, and I'd like to see that put to good use, not frittered away because you aren't like everyone else."

"Can't argue with that," Ned said as Crispin gaped.

Day's golden eyes switched to him. "I'm glad you agree with me, Mr. Hall. I rather want you as well."

"You what? What do you mean, me?"

"Well, you're a problem," Mrs. Gold said. "You've got no powers, but now you have senses, which Dan, the doctor who saw you, doesn't think are going to go away. That means you're falling between two stools. You're not a practitioner, but you're in our world whether you like it or not, and we can't just leave you to go mad hearing things you don't understand. Well, we could, I suppose, but Steph and I are both rather impressed by the way you handled this business, and we're not particularly easy to impress."

"Exactly. There's an opportunity here." Day's eyes were bright. "You work well with Tredarloe. You've got hearing, he's got powers, you've got sense, and the pair of you have *communication*. I'd like to see if we could use you."

"Hold on, hold on." Ned had both his hands up. "I'm a wasteman, remember?"

"Yes," Day said. "Is that all you want to be?"

"Excuse *me*," Crispin said indignantly. "That's Ned's business you're talking about, and it's blasted hard work."

"Don't think he could do it?"

"He could do anything he wants!" Crispin said, walking right into that one. "But he's not a practitioner. How would it be safe—"

"You two managed yesterday," Mrs. Gold said. "We'd have to work around things, thrash out how this might be done, but I agree with Steph: you make a good team and there isn't enough common sense floating around these halls that we can afford to waste any. You'd still have to do the devil of a lot of training, Tredarloe. We can't have you disarmed if someone takes your pencil case away."

"But in theory," Day said. "In theory. What do you think?"

Ned glanced at Crispin, who looked entirely bewildered. "Is this an offer or an order? I mean, does he get to say no, and what happens if he does?"

"Offer," said Mrs. Gold. "If he says no, we'll have to go back to the Council for another endless meeting, and I dare say that idiot Maupert will put his tuppence worth in again. I'll be honest, Tredarloe, I think things might be tiresome if you refuse. Then again, being a justiciar is ghastly, thankless, dangerous, and badly paid, so it's probably much of a muchness."

"And on that note…" Day stood. "Go home and think about it, please. Give us a decision tomorrow. Esther, take Hall out, would you? I want a quick word with Tredarloe."

CHAPTER THIRTEEN

It wasn't far from Lincoln's Inn Fields to Grape Street. They walked back along High Holborn, without consultation, both sets of feet turning that way. High Holborn was choked with hansom cabs, carts, and carriages, the pavements a jostling mass of humanity buying and selling, shouting, stealing, or simply going home. There was no way they could speak on that road, and so they didn't.

They bought grub as they walked—coffee, pies, stodgy-sweet slabs of plum dough—and walked together down Grape Street to where the door of the rag'n'bottle stood open.

Ned clicked his tongue. "Drat. S'pose it needed clearing out."

"Sorry. I didn't have a key."

"Eh. Not much to steal in there anyway."

All the more saleable metal items had gone, but the shop at least hadn't been despoiled or wrecked, more than had happened in Ned's brief skirmish with Dr. Sweet. "I suppose it could have been worse?" Crispin offered, looking around. "They must have been very careful burglars."

Burglars indeed. It would be the people of Grape Street, who well knew Voake had left no family and had mouths of their own to feed. "Ah, it's fair enough. Finders keepers." Ned frowned. "I'll be narked if they went into the store, though."

The finding and keeping had not been so incautious as to trespass on Ned's turf. His part of the building was quite untouched.

"Helps to have nothing to steal." He bolted both sets of doors and turned. "So. That was fun. What shall we do now?"

Crispin started to laugh. He whooped with it until he had to sit down on a stack of paper to keep his balance, and it set Ned off as well, the ridiculousness of it bubbling through him. He slid to the floor and thumped his head against Crispin's legs, shoulders heaving.

"Jumping Judas," Crispin said at last, wiping his eyes. "Honestly, Ned."

"What a day." Ned tipped his head back against the warm thigh behind him, still grinning. He could see Crispin watching him, his eyes shining with tears of laughter and warm with more, and felt his chest tighten in the most absurd way. "So what d'you think? Going to take it?"

He didn't have to say what *it* was. Crispin made a face. "I don't quite know. It's not what I'd have wanted to do. I mean, they deal with criminals and murderers and warlocks. I don't know if I could do that."

"Don't you?"

"Well, I could, obviously, because I did. *We* did. But..." He trailed off.

"But?"

"They want me," Crispin said slowly. "And they want my talents, and they think I could do a good job. They think I'd do the right thing."

Which sounded fine to Ned, but he thought he could take a stab at what was putting that little crease between Crispin's eyes. "You're not used to people thinking that, are you?"

"No, I'm not, except for you. You've thought that since the day we met, even when I got everything wrong."

"You never got everything wrong," Ned said. "I mean, you ain't always got everything right, but that's not the same thing."

"It feels like that, though. To me." Crispin swallowed. "I've always…been afraid, really. That you had me all wrong and that when you finally realised I'm just not as, as impressive as you seem to think, you wouldn't like it. Me."

"You know what your problem is?" Ned asked.

"What?"

"You're daft as a brush. Come here." He tugged Crispin's hand until he slipped down to the floor on a whispering rush of paper and they were both leaning on elbows, facing one another. "You're pretty impressive, no joke. You're magic. But that's not the bit I like. No denying I'd be happier if you were a normal bloke—" Crispin's face clouded. Ned tugged his hair gently. "Can't be helped. And anyway, it's not only the magic, it's…" This stuff was no fun at all, but if he didn't say it now, he never would. "Well, *you* reckon you don't feel like much, sometimes?" He ran his hand over Crispin's face, thumb tracing his elegant cheekbones, the curve of his lips. "You're a marvel. You got powers, and education, and those blooming freckles. Me? All I've got is a lot of paper dust."

"Oh, don't be ridiculous." Crispin looked actually shocked. "You can't think that. You've got a business, you manage things, you can do anything you turn your hand to. You're so good at—at *living*. Honestly, Ned. If I was stupid enough not to see that, see *you*, I'd deserve everything I got." He slipped his hand through the crook of Ned's arm, reaching for his face to match his movements. "*And* you're a stunner. Paper dust, indeed. What nonsense."

Ned's face felt so hot the paper he lounged on was in danger of catching ablaze. He hadn't been fishing for compliments, as such, just trying to make things clear, but the look in Crispin's eyes was enough to bring anyone to his knees. "You saying I'm not dusty?"

Crispin gave a sideways sort of shrug. "No denying I'd be happier if you didn't make me sneeze," he mimicked in quite respectable Cockney.

Ned smiled against his fingers. "Maybe I'll make you do more than sneeze."

"Maybe you should." Crispin pushed a finger gently but meaningfully between Ned's lips, and Ned caught it and sucked. Crispin grunted responsively, eyes half-closing. Ned scooted over, not releasing him, and rolled Crispin onto his back. He liked to take the lead, and Ned liked to let him, but he wanted a go at his lover, a chance to remind them both of everything that had seemed to be tumbling away from them a few days back.

He propped himself on one elbow and got his other hand to work, roaming over Crispin's chest, pushing his coat aside, finding his nipples through the cloth of his shirt and teasing each to hardness in turn. Crispin's eyes were shut, mouth open, lips pink, and his finger was twitching as Ned gave it the sort of seeing-to that ought to put ideas in his head. And clearly did, because he could see the jerk of Crispin's hips, bringing his arousal to Ned's attention.

Time enough. He trailed his fingers down to the inviting waistband, paused just to get a moan, and then set his hand nice and snug between Crispin's legs.

"Mmph! Ned…"

His prick was hard and solid in Ned's palm, and he rolled that gently, a tiny movement, pressing with the heel of his hand, nudging Crispin's balls rhythmically with his fingers. Crispin squirmed in a pleasurable agony of anticipation and opened his eyes to look into Ned's with such a smile, such a look, that all his plans for a teasing mouth-fuck evaporated.

"Oh, Freckles," he mumbled. Crispin pulled his finger out with a wet pop, and Ned more or less fell forward onto him, lips hitting lips as Crispin's fingers gripped the back of his skull. They kissed as if for breath, pushing against one another with sudden urgency, wrapped around one another. Ned's hand was trapped between both sets of hips, and he heaved his arse up a bit and did some hasty fumbling with buttons, without breaking the kiss. He needed to be kissing Crispin.

Crispin's hands on him were as needy as Ned felt. He was stroking and clutching like he wanted all of Ned at once, wrapping his legs around Ned's thighs. Ned rocked against him and shoved linen aside to get Crispin's prick out, springing free in the limited space to meet Ned's own. He worked his hand round them both, Crispin's feeling almost as familiar as his own after all these months, wrapping them together, running his thumb over the tops and down. Crispin was making little noises of pleasure in his mouth as they moved, finding a rhythm. Moans, harsh breaths, a hum of magic in Ned's ears, the rustle of clothing against the urgent movement of his hand. And the rub of Crispin's smooth, strong prick against his own, just right, applying the perfect pressure as Ned kept them held close. His hand was wet with the spill from Crispin's cock, or his own, or both. Crispin's arm was around his neck, his tongue in Ned's mouth, his legs round his back, both of them holding and held, and one last thrust and rub was all it took. Ned cried out, and felt his own spend and Crispin's pulse wet against his palm.

He collapsed over Crispin, gasping, fighting off the drowsiness that always overtook him after the crisis. He didn't want to fall asleep now.

After a moment, Crispin gave him an only partly playful shove. Ned rolled off sideways and onto his back, and they lay, just breathing, smelling spunk and sweat and paper. Ned put his clean hand out and Crispin took it, lacing their fingers together.

He might have drifted off for a bit then, actually.

"Ned." Crispin was giving him a nudge.

"Mmm?"

"Wake up or go to bed."

"Mph." He blinked himself awake. "Come with me?"

"In a minute. I wanted to ask first. What about you? Would you consider it?"

Ned stifled a yawn. "What, the work? Depends on you. You don't want to take it up, I'm having nothing to do with it."

"Suppose I wanted to," Crispin said carefully. "Suppose I was going to take it up whether you wanted to or not. What would you do?"

Ned lay quiet for a while. There was an obvious question, which he hadn't wanted to ask at the time, because he didn't plan to look uncertain in front of the justiciary if he could help it, but it needed raising. "You got many of my colour in your lot?"

"Some. Not many. Well, there aren't that many of us, really."

"I'll wager there's none in the justiciary."

"No."

Ned pulled a face. "Strikes me that's a problem right there."

"I tell you what, I *bet* Mr. Day and Mrs. Gold have thought about that," Crispin said. "There are a lot of practitioners who don't like taking orders from women, and they jolly well do it or Mrs. Gold asks why."

"Yeah, you wouldn't want that. But she can turn 'em into frogs or what-have-you. I'm not magic."

"Yes, well, I am," Crispin said, with a hint of bite in his voice. "And the justiciars watch out for each other. You saw that last night. The person who hurt Saint isn't going to get away."

"Right." Ned turned that over. "Well, it's a thought, I suppose. If I'm going to hear stuff anyway. And if there's something that can be done. It's too late to help poor old Voake and Reed, but if a chap could stop that happening next time… Plus, if there's a bit of extra treacle to stick to my fingers, I wouldn't grumble."

"What?"

"Money," Ned said patiently. "They said the pay wasn't good, but I'll wager it's better than a penny a pound on waste, and with less heavy lifting."

"We could see each other more, as well," Crispin added. "We'd have a reason. But, Ned, it's dangerous. I don't want to be a coward about this, and it wouldn't always be like last night, obviously. But still."

"True enough. But I saw enough men go to smash on the docks. Docks, trains, factories, they're none of 'em safe, are they?"

"Or the mines, or fishing." Crispin sighed. "I always wanted to do something lovely and safe with books, and look what happened."

"They get you coming and going," Ned agreed. "So what do you think?"

Crispin sat up, tugging Ned's hand till he grunted and sat up as well. "What I think is, I want to be with you. I want to feel like the kind of person who *deserves* to be with you. I know you think I'm all right, but, well, I've got to think that too. And we did something last night, didn't we? We stopped a monster. Two, really. We saved lives. So…" He took a deep breath. "I think I'm going to try, unless there's something you haven't said." He leaned forward until he and Ned were bumping noses. "But if there's any reason at all you don't like it, I want you to tell me, because doing the right thing for me means doing the right thing for us. Yes?"

Ned blew out a breath, making the flop of hair over Crispin's eyes jump and dance. "Almost. Except the bit where you've to prove anything to me, or anyone else."

"I know."

"But I reckon you're right. If you got to be a magician—a practitioner—you might as well be the kind that stops nasty business. Better that than the kind that does it."

"Ah," Crispin said. "That, er, that reminds me."

Ned shifted back a little, giving him a suspicious look. "Reminds you?"

"Well." Crispin reached for his discarded jacket and delved into a pocket. "The thing is, what Mr. Day wanted me for…"

Ned looked at what he held out. "Oh, you're *joking*."

"It's for you," Crispin said hastily. "To write with, I mean, the way we did yesterday. And if we can find another way to do that, or you don't want it, we can always throw it back in the river. It's up to you."

Ned plucked the silver pen from his fingers. "For me. Not you?"

"Not me," Crispin said. "I'd have left it in the Thames. I've no idea how Mr. Day got it out. But if you're going to be putting yourself in harm's way, I'd like you to have it. In case."

Ned contemplated the pen. It wasn't like he'd be tempted to use it lightly; he could still feel remembered pain in the back of his neck. "Well. All right. You won't want it?"

Crispin looked at the floor. "I don't think so. It was easy without, when I had to."

That should have sounded more cheerful than it did, Ned couldn't help feeling. "Was it?"

"Drawing the warlock, writing it dead. It was so *easy*."

Ned pulled him over, getting him close. "So you can do that. Doesn't mean you will, does it? What, you think I'm going to hide behind doors and wallop people with sticks all the time because I've done it once?"

Crispin spluttered into his shoulder. Ned tightened his grip. "Look, you're all right. I don't know where this is going, or how it'll work out, but I'll give it a try if you will. Like the man said, we work pretty well together."

"We do, don't we?" Crispin lifted his head with a smile.

Ned kissed the top of his nose. "It's been a long day, and a long night before that. How about we sleep on it?"

"I need to eat something first. After that, maybe I could find a way to make you sleepy?"

Crispin's eyes were bright, and full of mischief and hope, and something more than that. And he was right here, in Ned's paper store, with a future spooling out in front of them both—heaven knew what kind of future, but it was more than he'd ever thought or dreamed— and if Ned had been one of those chaps in the melodramas, he'd probably have been bursting out into song right about now.

"Sounds good," he agreed instead. "Yeah, you take care of that, Freckles. I reckon tomorrow can take care of itself."

Thanks for reading! If you want to know how Ned and Crispin met, check out the short story *A Queer Trade*.

Stephen Day's story begins with *The Magpie Lord*.

The Magpie Lord
A Charm of Magpies book 1
A lord in danger. A magician in turmoil. A snowball in hell.

Exiled to China for twenty years, Lucien Vaudrey never planned to return to England. But with the mysterious deaths of his father and brother, it seems the new Lord Crane has inherited an earldom. He's also inherited his family's enemies. He needs magical assistance, fast. He doesn't expect it to turn up angry.

Magician Stephen Day has good reason to hate Crane's family. Unfortunately, it's his job to deal with supernatural threats. Besides, the earl is unlike any aristocrat he's ever met, with the tattoos, the attitude... and the way Crane seems determined to get him into bed. That's definitely unusual.

Soon Stephen is falling hard for the worst possible man, at the worst possible time. But Crane's dangerous appeal isn't the only thing rendering Stephen powerless. Evil pervades the house, a web of plots is closing round Crane, and if Stephen can't find a way through it— they're both going to die.

Jonah Pastern and Ben Spenser's story is told in *Jackdaw*.

Jackdaw
A Charm of Magpies linked story
If you stop running, you fall.

Jonah Pastern is a magician, a liar, a windwalker, a professional thief…and for six months, he was the love of police constable Ben Spenser's life. His betrayal left Ben jailed, ruined, alone, and looking for revenge.

Ben is determined to make Jonah pay. But he can't seem to forget what they once shared, and Jonah refuses to let him. Soon Ben is entangled in Jonah's chaotic existence all over again, and they're running together—from the police, the justiciary, and some dangerous people with a lethal grudge against them.

Threatened on all sides by betrayals, secrets, and the laws of the land, the policeman and the thief must find a way to live and love before the past catches up with them...

THE CHARM OF MAGPIES SERIES

Series reading order is as follows

A Charm of Magpies (Stephen Day and Lord Crane)
    The Magpie Lord
    Interlude with Tattoos (short story)
    A Case of Possession
    A Case of Spirits (short story)
    Flight of Magpies
    Feast of Stephen (short story)

Each book is published with its companion story. 'The Smuggler and the Warlord', a very short early story of Crane and Merrick in China, is available free on my website at kjcharleswriter.com.

The Charm of Magpies World
    Jackdaw
    A Queer Trade (Rag and Bone prequel)
    Rag and Bone

These are standalone stories with different couples taking place in the same world. *A Queer Trade* is set in the summer of *A Case of Possession*; *Jackdaw* and *Rag and Bone* are both set in the spring following *Flight of Magpies*.

BOOKS BY KJ CHARLES

A Charm of Magpies series
The Magpie Lord
A Case of Possession
Flight of Magpies
Jackdaw
A Queer Trade
Rag and Bone

Society of Gentlemen series
The Ruin of Gabriel Ashleigh
A Fashionable Indulgence
A Seditious Affair
A Gentleman's Position

Sins of the Cities series
An Unseen Attraction
An Unnatural Vice
An Unsuitable Heir

Standalone books
Think of England
The Secret Casebook of Simon Feximal
Wanted, a Gentleman

Green Men
Spectred Isle

ABOUT THE AUTHOR

KJ Charles is a writer and editor. She lives in London with her husband, two kids, a garden with quite enough prickly things, and a cat with murder management issues.

KJ is represented by Courtney Miller-Callihan.

Find her at www.kjcharleswriter.com for book info and blogging, on Twitter @kj_charles for daily timewasting and the odd rant, or in her Facebook group, KJ Charles Chat, for sneak peeks and special extras.